CAPTAIN JAMES KIRK: Absolute master of the largest and most modern vessel in the Starfleet service, *USS Enterprise*, and of the manifold talents of the 430 highly trained crewmen; his decisions alone can affect the future course of civilisation throughout the universe.

SCIENCE OFFICER SPOCK: First Officer of the *Enterprise* and, it is said, best First Officer in the whole fleet; his knowledge of computers is total and his mental abilities indispensable. Half Vulcan, half human by birth, Spock is logical to the exclusion of all emotion – except curiosity!

DR BONES McCOY: Senior Ship's Surgeon and expert in space psychology, McCoy at times appears to be the traditional 'witch doctor' of space as he combats the deadliest and virulent of maladies – whether physical or mental – from all manner of worlds and species with baffling ease!

Also in the *Star Trek* series

STAR TREK 1
STAR TREK 2
STAR TREK 3
STAR TREK 4
STAR TREK 5
STAR TREK 6
STAR TREK 7
STAR TREK 8
STAR TREK 9
STAR TREK 10
STAR TREK 11
SPOCK MUST DIE
SPOCK MESSIAH
TREK TO MADWORLD
VULCAN!
THE STARLESS WORLD
DEVIL WORLD

and published by Corgi Books

Star Trek 12

Adapted by James Blish and J. A. Lawrence

Based on the exceiting
television series
created by Gene Roddenberry

CORGI BOOKS

STAR TREK 12

A CORGI BOOK 0 552 10759 X

First publication in Great Britain

PRINTING HISTORY
Corgi edition published 1978
Corgi edition reissued 1985

Corgi Books are published by Transworld Publishers Ltd.,
Century House, 61-63 Uxbridge Road,
Ealing, London W5 5SA.

Made and printed in Great Britain by
Hunt Barnard Printing Ltd., Aylesbury, Bucks.

CONTENTS

Foreword   vii
Preface   ix

PATTERNS OF FORCE   1
THE GAMESTERS OF TRISKELION   34
AND THE CHILDREN SHALL LEAD   74
THE CORBOMITE MANEUVER   103
SHORE LEAVE   140

Appendix I   171
Appendix II   175

FOREWORD

As some of you may know, James Blish died on July 30, 1975.

Star Trek 12 was almost completed. So many letters! We couldn't disappoint everybody by leaving this series unfinished. So Mr. Roddenberry, Bantam Books and Paramount all very kindly agreed that I could write up the last two scripts—"Shore Leave" and "And the Children Shall Lead"—so we could get this book to all of you who have asked for it, with apologies for the delay.

The two appendices in the back, which list the episodes of this series, were suggested by Miss Gail A. Piedmont, to whom many thanks for the idea.

You may perhaps wonder about the two stories concerning Harry Mudd—"Mudd's Women" and "I, Mudd." Mr. Blish did indeed write these, but he planned to extend them to novel length, with some additional adventures. So in fear and trepidation, I am tackling that too, and it will be along presently.

Please, everybody, neither Mr. Blish nor I ever had the privilege of meeting the actors, much less could we obtain their autographs for you. And now Mr. Blish's own autograph is unobtainable. If you want pictures and other materials, write to Star Trek Enterprises, P.O. Box 38429, Hollywood, California 90038.

In *Star Trek 3,* Mr. Blish explained why he had to return some manuscripts from readers unread. Please note again that it is not possible to even look at them, partly for legal reasons; moreover, it is very frustrating to have to send them right back to you. He suggested that writing original science fiction and sending your stories to the magazines would be easier and more rewarding than writing scripts for an existing television program.

Thank you for all your many letters. James enjoyed reading them very much. Many of you ask why he wrote science fiction. He liked to, that's why! (So do I.) Live long and prosper.

Judith A. Lawrence
(Mrs. James Blish)

Athens
February 1977

PREFACE

It's question time again, so without further ado:

A number of you have asked me how I came to write these adaptations in the first place. The answer is simple and unglamorous: Bantam Books asked me to, out of the blue as it were. I had no connections with *Star Trek* and hadn't even written a script for the show, though several friends of mine had. I had seen the pilot film at a science-fiction convention and had watched the show on television, but my only real qualifications were first, that I had written about two dozen other science-fiction books, including a Hugo winner; and second, that I had also written television and film scripts.

I took on the job to see if I would like it, for one book. I did; and, furthermore, your letters convinced me that you made up a huge new audience for science fiction, one that had never been reached by the specialized magazines (and more often than not had been put off by the monster movies that had been Hollywood's usual caricature of science fiction). The rest is history—thirteen books of it now. Whew.

How many more will I write? I hope to go on until I've used up all the scripts. There may also be another *ST* novel.

I have very often been asked why my adaptations sometimes differ in some respects from the shows as actually shown. (Apparently many of you tape-record the broadcasts, or own copies of the scripts or have them by heart.) About one letter in every ten poses this question, a few of them quite indignantly. The answer to that is a little more complex:

1. The scripts that I have to work from are theoretically shooting scripts, or final drafts, and I almost always try to be as faithful to their texts as length permits. Sometimes, however, there seem to have been last-minute changes made which are not reflected in my copies.

2. *Star Trek* people have frequently reported that brand new speeches, bits of business and so on were occasionally introduced during the actual production and filmed without ever having been written down formally. Obviously, no existing script would show these, although transcripts would catch a few.

3. Television and the printed word are in some respects quite different media, and this shows up especially sharply in science fiction, where more often than not it's necessary to explain the technical or scientific reasons behind what is going on. A television show simply cannot stop the action for detailed explanations; but I can work such explanations into a story version, and I do when I think it's necessary.

4. On one occasion—and one only—the ending of a show just did not seem to me to make much sense when reduced to cold typescript, though it went over well enough on the tube. I worked out a new ending which I thought would stand up better to re-reading, and asked Paramount's permission to make the change, which they readily granted. I repeat, I did this only once, and long ago; it's not a privilege I mean to abuse.

Thank you again for your letters; I only wish I could answer them.

James Blish

STAR TREK 12

PATTERNS OF FORCE
(John Meredyth Lucas)

Officially, the mission was location of a missing cultural observer assigned to Ekos, sister planet of Zeon in a double system. But both Kirk and Spock had personal interest invested in the whereabouts of John Gill. The missing man had been Kirk's instructor at the Space Academy. As to Spock, he'd studied his Earth history from a John Gill text. Now, as the *Enterprise* entered into orbit around Ekos, the inner planet, the two men looked at the distinguished face projected onto the bridge screen.

Kirk remembered it well. "Lieutenant Uhura, try to raise John Gill on Starfleet communication channels."

"Aye, sir."

"Jim, Starfleet's been trying for six months," McCoy said. "If he's still alive, isn't it unlikely he'd receive us now?"

"I don't know, Doctor. We're here to find out what's happened *because* I don't know."

"No response on any Starfleet channel, Captain," Uhura reported.

Spock, his eyes still on the screen, said, "What impressed me most was Gill's treatment of history as causes and motivations rather than dates and events. His text was—"

Chekov interrupted. "Spacecraft approaching from the inner planet, Captain."

"From Ekos?"

1

The question sent Spock back to his station. Checking his own viewer, he said, "Yes, Captain. But it must be a Zeon ship. The Zeons have a crude interplanetary capability." He leaned closer to his viewer. "Reaction powered. A small rocket. And it's on an intercept course." He lifted his head to look at Kirk. "That means sophisticated detection equipment that neither Zeon nor Ekos should have."

Kirk, nodding, swung his chair to Uhura. "Try ship-to-ship frequencies, Lieutenant."

Spock spoke again. "No indication of life aboard, Captain. It's an unmanned probe which seems to be carrying a warhead."

Kirk spoke, "Standby phasers, Mr. Chekov."

"Phasers ready, sir."

"Range, Mr. Chekov?"

"Two hundred kilometers, sir. Closing fast."

"Fire," Kirk said.

John Gill's face vanished from the screen. In its stead, a blue-white flare of light flashed. The bridge trembled under shock waves.

"A thermonuclear warhead," Spock said.

McCoy stared at him. "But that's generations away from where these people should be technologically! How could they have managed nuclear physics?"

Kirk, recalling the brilliant eyes of John Gill, said, "Maybe they had help."

It was unthinkable. But a Starship Captain had to oblige himself to think the unthinkable. The ugly fact remained that John Gill's Ekos had launched attack on the *Enterprise*. "Mr. Chekov, plot us a maximum orbit. Let's get out of their detection equipment's range."

"Orbit computed and locked in, sir."

"Execute."

As the impulse engines came on, Scott emerged from the elevator and Uhura said, "Still no response from John Gill on any channel, sir."

"He must be dead," McCoy said. "And what's going on down there on Ekos?"

Spock looked up. "According to our records, the

Ekosians are warlike, primitive, in a state of anarchy. Zeon, the other planet, has a relatively high technology, and its people are peaceful."

Kirk got up to go to the computer station. "You're saying that the people with the war potential aren't warlike, Mr. Spock. So who threw that missile at us?"

"Our computer data appear to be considerably out of date, Captain. Obviously, things have been happening very rapidly on Ekos."

Kirk took a brief pace of the bridge. "Mr. Spock, we've run into something more disturbing than John Gill's disappearance. You and I will beam down to Ekos."

Scott said, "After what they just threw at us, I suggest a landing party in force, sir."

"No. We'll observe the non-interference directive, Scotty."

"Jim," McCoy said, "I think he's got a good—"

"All right. We'll take one precaution. Bones, prepare subcutaneous transponders in the event we're unable to use our communicators."

"Captain, may I suggest the ship's uniform section prepare clothing suitable to the culture?"

"You may indeed, Mr. Spock."

McCoy performed the simple operation in the Transporter Room. His patients had changed into nondescript denim work clothes, Spock wearing a stocking cap to hide his ears. Rolling up a sleeve, Kirk said, "All right, Doctor, insert the transponders." McCoy used a hypo to inject the tiny devices into their left wrists. They rolled down their sleeves to cover the small bumps. Then Kirk spoke to Scott.

"Make one low pass to communication range in three hours, Scotty. If we fail to make contact at the appointed time, take our coordinates from the transponders—and beam us aboard, whatever our condition might be."

Scott was glum. "Aye, Captain. Whatever your condition."

The two stepped onto the platform.

3

"Energize," Kirk said.

Scott moved dials. The Transporter shimmer sparkled.

"Good luck!" McCoy shouted.

But they were gone.

The time on Ekos was day, and the place they arrived in was a street—a street appropriate to an Earth of the Twentieth Century. Looking around him, Spock said, "The Ekosians are humanoid, so there is apt to be a certain similarity in structure. It is interesting how body form tends to shape the structure of—"

"Mr. Spock, we're not here to do an architectural study. We are—"

Kirk broke off at sudden shouts and the sound of running feet. A young man, clearly spent and terrified, raced around the corner to their left, all his strength centered on his effort to elude his pursuers. He was almost on top of the *Enterprise* men before he saw them. "Hide!" he panted. "They are right behind me! Quickly! Get away . . ."

He sank to his knees, his lungs heaving. The shouting behind him grew louder. Spock pulled Kirk into the shadow of a doorway as three armed men rounded the corner. They wore the brown shirts of Nazi Storm Troopers, their left arms encircled by black bands marked with red circles. In the center of each circle was a black swastika.

"There's the Zeon pig!"

They surrounded the kneeling man. "On your feet, pig!" One of the troopers kicked the man. It was a good game. The others joined in it.

Kirk's hand had instinctively reached for his phaser. Spock checked him. "The non-interference directive, Captain."

"Hands over your head, Zeon. Higher!"

The man's mouth was bleeding. Gratified by sight of the blood, the biggest trooper yelled, "Keep those hands in the air! Don't touch anything Ekosian! You swine have defiled us enough! Move!" He planted a heavy foot in the man's back and sent him sprawling. Then his victim was jerked to his feet to be marched away.

The horrified Kirk spoke to Spock. "It's a nightmare. Did you recognize those uniforms? That armband?"

"Mid-Twentieth Century Earth. A nation state called Nazi Germany, Captain."

"Attention! Attention! Attention!"

The newscaster's voice came from a loudspeaker set on a post a few yards away. As its square TV screen lighted up, the voice said, "An announcer from Führer Headquarters. . . ."

A brown-shirted announcer, a flag bearing the Nazi emblem behind him, appeared on the screen. "Today," he said, "the Führer has ordered our glorious capital made Zeon free. Starting at dawn, our heroic troops began flushing out the Zeon monsters who have been poisoning our planet. . . ."

His face was replaced by the spectacle of burly SS men rounding up a group of pitifully frightened old men, women and children. One of the children was crying.

Watching, Kirk said, "How could this have happened? The chance of another planet developing a Nazi culture, using the forms, symbols, the uniforms of Twentieth Century Earth, is so fantastically slim that—"

Spock interrupted. "Virtually impossible, Captain. Yet the evidence is quite clear."

The screen was now showing shots of a panzer column and troops goose-stepping under the roar of Stuka dive bombers. The uniformed announcer's voice was saying, "The Führer's Headquarters reports repulsing an attack by Zeon spacecraft. Our missiles utterly destroyed the enemy."

Kirk turned to Spock. "The 'enemy' would have been the *Enterprise*. You look well, Mr. Spock, for having been utterly destroyed." He looked back at the screen. It now held the image of a vast amphitheater, massed with thousands upon thousands of cheering troops. Over the noise, the announcer said, "At this patriotic demonstration, Deputy Führer Melakon presented the iron cross, second class, to Daras, Hero of the Fatherland."

The scene changed to a close-up of a cold-faced, middle-aged man in uniform, flanked by Gestapo guards. A girl mounted the podium, wearing her uniform with grace and style. Under its cap her blonde hair gleamed with a light of its own. Her beautiful face was grave with pride as Melakon pinned the decoration to the breast of her uniform.

The announcer was back. He came to rigid attention as he spoke. "Everywhere, preparations go forward for the final decision. Death to Zeon! Long live the Fatherland!"

The TV camera left his face to focus on a huge poster on the wall behind him. Framed in black and red, its four corners were decorated with swastikas. It held a portrait.

"Long live the Führer!" the announcer shouted, and, turning, gave the portrait a stiff-armed salute.

The face in the portrait was that of John Gill.

Older—but unmistakable.

Kirk was stunned. "That's John Gill! The Führer!"

"Fascinating!" Spock exclaimed.

"You there!"

They wheeled. They were facing an SS Lieutenant. The trooper's Luger was leveled at Kirk's stomach. "Zeons!" he cried. Then his eyes narrowed as he took another look at Spock. He whipped off the stocking cap with a yell of triumph. "What are those, ears? What kind of monsters are the Zeons sending against us?"

Kirk caught Spock's eye. He signaled, and, stepping away from him, induced the SS man to turn slightly. "You're right, Lieutenant," he said. "He is not one of us."

"What do you mean 'us'?"

"Lieutenant, look out!"

Spock timed his warning to a sideways leap. The officer's eyes followed him, centering on him just long enough for Kirk to move. He chopped him. The Lieutenant dropped.

Kirk nodded to Spock. As they stripped the man of his uniform, Kirk said, "His helmet will conceal your 'monster' ears, Mr. Spock."

"You propose that we pass ourselves off as Nazis, sir?"

"If John Gill is the leader, this would seem the 'logical' way to approach him."

Shouldering into the uniform coat, Spock said, "A point well taken, Captain." Kirk eyed him in his full SS uniform. "Somewhat gaudy, Mr. Spock. But I think it's an improvement."

Spock threw him a look of disgust. Cautiously, they edged out into the street. But their care didn't pay off. This time it was a Gestapo Lieutenant who accosted them. He had grabbed Kirk's shoulder, but as he recognized Spock's uniform, he let it go.

"A Zeon?"

Spock nodded. "I captured him. Is that not the proper procedure with enemies of the Fatherland?"

"With all Zeon pigs, Lieutenant."

"Take charge of him," Spock said.

"With pleasure." He seized Kirk again. "All right, Zeon, today we have a surprise for you. We—"

He collapsed under the Vulcan neck pinch. Kirk looked down at the unconscious body. "I'm sorry, Spock, that your uniform isn't as attractive as mine is. I believe this is the Gestapo variety."

"Correct, Captain. You should make a very convincing Nazi."

Kirk snapped him a look. But he was too busy turning himself into a Gestapo officer to think of a suitable rejoinder.

They gave themselves time before mounting the steps of the Chancellery. Swastikas were everywhere—on the banners that fluttered over the building, on the armbands of the SS men who stood at its massive doors, armed with submachine guns. The guards snapped to attention as an SS General Officer crossed the pavement to the steps. Kirk and Spock played it cool as they followed behind him. An SS Major came out of the big doors as the General entered them.

The Major glared at Spock. "Lieutenant! Have you forgotten how to salute?"

Spock extended his arm in a crisp Nazi salute.

"Papers," the Major said.

Kirk turned to Spock. "Your orders, Lieutenant. The Major wants to see your orders. There, in your jacket . . ."

The Major studied them suspiciously as Spock reached quickly into his jacket. He came out with a wallet, and the Major took it.

Kirk moved into the obvious breach of confidence. "The Lieutenant is a little dazed, sir. He captured several Zeons single-handed. But one of the pigs struck him before he dropped. I promise you, that pig will never get up again."

"Good work, Lieutenant. Hail the Führer!"

He handed the wallet back to Spock. Kirk quickly extended his arm in the Nazi salute. "Hail the Führer!"

Spock repeated the litany. "Hail the Führer!"

"This is a day to remember, Major," Kirk said.

As they passed into the Chancellery, the Major stopped Spock, solicitude in his face. "Better have a doctor check you, Lieutenant. You don't look well. Your color is— Remove your helmet."

"We have no time to waste," Spock said.

Kirk's heart was pounding. "Major, we have urgent business with the Führer. We must see him immediately."

The Major was inexorable. "Your helmet, Lieutenant. Take it off!"

The guards' submachine guns jabbed brutally into Spock's neck. He lifted the helmet, revealing his pointed Vulcan ears.

In the cell, they had stripped Kirk to the waist. For a purpose. They did nothing without a purpose. The naked, uncovered flesh made the whip's lashing immediate. Like Spock, manacled too, he made no sound as the whip cut bloody grooves into his back. Behind them in the cell, the Zeon they had first seen brutalized lay, retching, on his stomach.

"You wish to talk now?"

The SS Major was pleased to be irritated. "Tell me your orders! You were sent to kill our Führer. Confess! Do you want some more persuasion?"

Kirk rallied the power of speech. "You're making this a rather one-sided conversation, Major."

"Don't joke with me, Zeon pig!" The Major glanced at his SS lasher. He took a lowered, confidential tone. "Who is this pointed-eared alien? Things will go easier with you if you tell me about him."

Kirk lifted his pain-filled eyes. "Let us talk to the Führer. We'll tell him anything he wants to know."

"You'll be glad to talk to *me* before I've finished with you, you Zeon swine, you—"

The cell door opened. A man, simply uniformed in Party dress but radiating an air of quiet, self-intact authority, walked in. The SS Major stiffened to awed attention. "Chairman Eneg! I am honored! Excellency, I have been interrogating these two spies, captured in the very act of—"

"I have had the full report."

The quiet man ignored the Major to speak to Spock. "You are not from Zeon. Where do you come from?"

Kirk said, "We'll explain when we see the Führer."

"And what is your business with the Führer?"

"We can discuss that only with him."

Furious, the Major seized the whip from the guard and slashed Kirk with it. "Pig! You're speaking to the Chairman of the Party!"

"That's enough, Major!" Eneg said sharply. He turned to Kirk. "What are the weapons that were found on you? What design?"

Kirk was silent. Eneg looked at the Major. "Our famously efficient SS laboratories have failed to discover how your weapons work."

The Major reddened. "Excellency, give me a few minutes with them, and I promise you I'll have them—"

"You've had more than a few minutes with them without result." Eneg looked at Kirk's slashed back. "The trouble with you SS people is that you don't realize punishment is ineffective after a certain point. Men become insensitive."

After a moment, the Major said, "Yes, Excellency."

"Lock them up. Let their pain argue with them. Then I will question them."

"Excellency, the standing order is: 'Interrogate and execute.' The interrogation is finished. Therefore—"

"Finished, Major? What have you learned? Nothing. Hold them for an hour."

"Excellency, the order—"

Eneg's quiet eyes flashed with sudden anger. "That is *my* order, Major. I suggest that you do not disobey it."

"Yes, Excellency."

Eneg turned to the door. The guard leaped to open it for him. As he left, the Major turned back to the *Enterprise* men. "All right, pigs. My eye will be on the clock. When the hour is up, you will die. Most unpleasantly, I promise you." He slammed the cell door behind him.

Slowly, the Zeon prisoner got to his feet, his eyes watchful as Spock said, "What do you propose to do, Captain?"

"I don't know. But we haven't much time to do it. Without our phasers . . . our communicators . . ." He looked around the cell. "John Gill is the only chance we have now."

"Captain, have you considered how he must have changed to be responsible for all this?"

"Professor Gill was one of the kindest, gentlest men I've ever known. For him to be a Nazi is so— It's just impossible."

The Zeon spoke. "Why did they take you? You are

not a Zeon." He nodded toward Spock. "And he certainly is not. Who are you?"

Spock said, "Why do the Nazis hate Zeons?"

The question evoked a bitter answer. "Without us to hate, there would be nothing to bring them together. So the Party has built us into a threat—a disease that must be wiped out."

"*Is* Zeon a threat to them?"

"Where *did* you come from? Our warlike period ended a dozen generations ago! When we came here, we thought we were civilizing the Ekosians!"

"Were they like this when you Zeons first came?" Kirk said.

"Warlike. But not vicious. That came after the Nazi movement started. Only a few years ago."

Spock looked at Kirk. "That would agree with the time of Gill's arrival, Captain."

The embittered Zeon was launched on the troubles of his people. "When they have destroyed us here, they will attack our planet with the technology we gave them. The danger is that the taking of life is so repugnant to us, we may go down without a struggle." His fists clenched. "After what I've seen in the streets today, I think *I* could kill!"

Kirk studied the impassioned face. "Do you know the plan of this building?"

The Zeon went on immediate guard. "Why?"

"If we can get to the SS weapons laboratory . . . get our weapons back, we can stop the slaughter of the Zeons."

"Why should you be interested in saving Zeons?" the man asked coldly.

Kirk turned back to Spock. "We must get our communicators and contact the ship."

"The flaw in that plan, Captain, is these locked cell doors. And beyond them is a guard."

"The transponders!" Kirk cried.

"Pardon, sir?"

But Kirk was staring at the cell's overhead light.

"A way to throw some light on our gloom, Mr. Spock!"

Spock looked thoughtfully at his wrist. "The rubidium crystals in the transponders! Of course, it would be crude, but perhaps workable. How can we get them out?"

They had lowered their voices. The Zeon hadn't heard their last exchange, but he continued to watch them, puzzled.

"Here," Kirk said.

He yanked the mattress from a bed, and, ripping the fabric, seized a wire spring. It snapped, its edge sharp. He used it to slit through the slight bulge on his wrist, releasing the bright red crystal. Blood welled from the cut. He handed the wire to Spock. As he too probed out his crystal, the Zeon cried, "You will kill yourselves? Bleed to death? But many do it to avoid the torture."

"That's not quite what we had in mind," Kirk told him. "You have the figures computed, Mr. Spock?"

"Yes, Captain. It will be necessary to hold the crystals at a specific distance. The distance should be two point seven millimeters. I shall put the first crystal . . ."

As he spoke, he placed a crystal into a hole at the edge of the flat spring, pushing it firmly in. ". . . here. The second one at the other end." He was bending the spring into a horseshoe shape so that the crystals at the two ends were precisely aligned. "Two point seven millimeters would be approximately here. That, of course, is a crude estimation."

The Zeon was staring in amazement. "What are you making—some kind of radio?"

"No. The electrical power in that light is very low, Mr. Spock."

"It should be sufficient to stimulate the rubidium crystal. As I recall from the history of Physics, the ancient lasers were able to achieve the necessary excitation, even using crude natural crystals. There. It's ready. But to reach the light source, I shall require a platform."

"I'd be honored, Mr. Spock." Kirk was wry, only too aware of his lacerated shoulders. He stooped under the bulb and Spock climbed up on them. "I'd appreciate it if you'd hurry, Mr. Spock. That guard did a very professional job with the whip."

Spock lifted the cylinder up to the bulb. "The aim, of course, can only be approximate," he said.

Kirk's shoulders were bleeding. "Spock, I'll settle if you can hit the broad side of a barn."

Spock frowned. "Why should I aim at such a structure, sir?"

"Never mind, Spock. Get on with the job."

The tiny rubidium crystals were glowing a bright red. Suddenly, ruby light flashed from Spock's contraption, cutting through the door's steel bars like butter. The lock was next. Kirk saw it loosen.

"All right, Mr. Spock. Don't overdo it."

Spock leaped from his shoulders. Kirk touched them, saw blood on his hand and wiped it off on the torn mattress fabric. The Zeon, awed, whispered, "What was that? Zeon science has nothing like it. With such a weapon, we'd have a chance against them!"

"It's not a weapon," Kirk said. "It has an extremely short range. Get over to that corner, Mr. Spock. Keep out of sight. I'll create a commotion."

At the cell door, he yelled, "All right. I'll talk. Please! I don't want to die. Guard! I'll talk. Call the Major. I'll talk!"

He shook the bars, still shouting. The guard took a half step forward. Spock jumped from his corner, thrust his hand through the bars and applied the neck pinch. The guard dropped. Spock opened the door, dragged the body into the cell and tossed the man's coat to Kirk. As Kirk struggled into it, the Zeon came out of his daze.

"Take me with you. Please give me a chance to fight them," he pleaded. "Take me—or you'll never find the laboratory."

"An excellent point, Mr. Spock. Take him. He's our guide."

13

But there was another guard in the corridor. Kirk pulled the gun from the downed man's holster, pressed it into the Zeon's back and, motioning Spock to get in front of him, lowered his voice. "Which door is the laboratory?"

"Second on the right," the Zeon whispered.

"All right, Zeon swine, move!" Kirk shouted.

The guard eyed them boredly and resumed his position. As they passed him, heading for the laboratory door, it opened. An SS Trooper emerged and, turning, locked the door behind him. He was walking by them when Kirk, jerking the Zeon toward him, shoved into the guard. They all fell back against a wall. Kirk slapped the Zeon.

"Clumsy Zeon pig!" He spoke to the guard. "Sorry, but these Zeons do nothing right. They'll pay for it though. They're on their way to the laboratory for experimental work." Nodding, the guard moved off. Grinning, Kirk held his keys.

The laboratory was deserted, but on a table to their left, Kirk spotted their disassembled communicators. He gathered up the parts.

"Who *are* you people?" the Zeon demanded.

"The phasers?" Kirk said.

"I do not see them, Captain."

"Where do you come from?" the Zeon asked again.

Kirk had discovered an informative clipboard. Flipping its pages, he read them hastily. Their phasers had been sent to Gestapo Command Headquarters for analysis. "We can forget about our phasers," he was telling Spock when the door was flung open. The SS Guard had learned that his keys were missing. He stared at Kirk and Spock, snapping his pistol up. The Zeon, out of his line of sight, struck him. The first blow was wild. But the second one dropped the trooper cold.

Kirk looked down at the felled man. "For peaceful people," he said, "you Zeons are very thorough."

They also learned quickly. The Zeon pointed to the

trooper's uniform. "Wearing that, we might be able to steal a car and get out of the capital."

"We came here to find John Gill," Kirk said.

Spock spoke. "Captain, without phasers, and until we are able to communicate with the ship, it is illogical to assume we can hold out against the entire military force of this planet."

Kirk considered the point. "All right, Mr. Spock. Get into that uniform and cover your ears again."

Within seconds, Spock was in full SS Lieutenant's regalia, his ears helmeted. Kirk, in the guard's outfit, found a stretcher piled on others in a corner of the laboratory. When they emerged from it, the Zeon lay on the stretcher, his eyes closed as though past an extremity of torture. The guard at the door snapped Spock a salute.

"Hunting's good," Kirk told him. "We've caught so many Zeons, we've got to dump them outside."

They got away with it. In the shadow of a building, they set the stretcher down. Spock said, "I suggest the guards will shortly notice our absence, Captain."

"There'll be a planet-wide alert," the Zeon warned them.

"We'll have to find someplace to hide until we can reassemble the communicators and get help from the *Enterprise*."

Kirk's remark seemed to deeply disturb the Zeon. He was clearly wrestling with some momentous decision.

"You could be spies," he said, "sent to find our underground hiding places." Then his face cleared. "But that's a chance I must take. I put my life in your hands. More important, I am putting the lives of our friends in your hands."

They followed him down the street, hugging the buildings' shadows until they came to a dark alley. It was dirty with a clutter of trash, garbage pails, a litter of empty tin cans. The Zeon went to the metal top of a manhole cover and rapped on it four times. Finally, from deep underground came the sound of four answering raps. The Zeon knocked at the manhole cover twice again, waving the two *Enterprise* men to a crouch as a patrol car, filled with troops, roared past the alley's entrance. When the noise had faded, the Zeon knocked again. The manhole cover lifted on a narrow, black opening.

"Come," said the Zeon.

A narrow metal ladder led down into the darkness. When they reached its last rung, a Zeon passed them and scrambled up to swing the metal cover shut again. He descended the ladder and their guide said, "Davod, you're well. How many are here?"

He wasn't answered. Davod was staring suspiciously at Kirk and Spock.

"They helped me escape from the prison! I owe them my life, Davod!"

"Isak!"

An older man, strong-faced, had entered the dim-lit room. "Abrom, thank God you're well." Their Zeon and the older man embraced. "This is my brother," their guide said. "Abrom, they were prisoners, beaten as I was."

Abrom's eyes were searching their faces. "Why were you in that prison?"

"I was trying to see the Führer," Kirk said.

"The Führer!"

"If I can see him, there may be a way to stop this insanity."

Isak said, "I owe them my life, Abrom."

Davod strode angrily out of the room and Abrom said, "Isak, Uletta is dead." After a moment, he added, "She was shot down in the street."

Isak's shocked face moved Kirk to ask, "Your sister?"

"She would have been my wife."

Abrom's voice shook. "She lived for five hours while they walked by her and spat on her. Our own people could do nothing to help. Yet you ask me to help strangers."

Isak lifted his face from the hands he had used to

16

hide it. "If we adopt the ways of the Nazis, we are as bad as the Nazis."

Spock, hesitating to intrude on such private tragedy, motioned Kirk aside. "Captain, may I suggest the most profitable use of our time would be to reassemble the communicators?" He spoke gently to Abrom. "May I work over there undisturbed for a few moments?"

Abrom didn't speak. Finally, Isak nodded, and taking his brother by the shoulder, moved away. Kirk joined Spock at a table where they spread out the communicators' elements. Using parts of both, Spock put one together, and, handing it to Kirk, said, "I cannot be certain that the circuits are correct. There's no way to test it except by actual use."

Kirk was about to remind him that the *Enterprise* would be beyond range for another hour when there were shouts and the sound of a shot outside. The door was burst open. Two Storm Troopers armed with submachine guns broke into the room. With them, her lovely head held arrogantly high, was the girl in brownshirt uniform they'd seen on the TV screen. She was wearing her iron cross.

Kirk remembered her name and her beauty.

"It's Daras," he told Spock.

"Quiet!" the girl shouted. "Over against the wall— all of you! Hands in the air, Zeon swine!"

She marched down the line of them, studying faces. Pausing when she came to Kirk, Spock and Isak, she said, "You are the three who escaped from the Chancellery. What was your plan?"

A gun aimed at Kirk. "Speak now!" she said. "It's the last chance you'll get!"

"I must see the Führer. It is urgent."

She seized a gun from a trooper. "Urgent? Yes, I'll bet it is!"

Abrom tried to distract her attention from Kirk. "I alone am responsible for what happens here."

"Do you know what we do with responsible Zeons?"

Her finger depressed the gun's trigger. There was a burst of fire and Abrom fell,

17

"Now we finish the job!" she cried.

A trooper swung his gun to cover Isak, Spock and Kirk.

Isak exploded in fury. "Where do you stop, you Nazis? When you've killed the last of us, what will you do then? Turn your guns on yourselves?"

Kirk met Spock's eyes in a signal. They ducked, then hurled themselves forward. Spock came up under a trooper's gun, and Kirk, hitting the weapon in Daras's hands, wrenched it away from her. He whirled with it, covering the three Nazis.

"Wait!" Isak yelled to him. "Don't shoot!"

Abrom had gotten to his feet. "No more," he said. "You've proved you're on our side."

Bewildered, Kirk turned to Isak, who met his eyes bravely. "Forgive me," he said. "We had to be sure."

Abrom put his hand on Kirk's arm. "Taking you in could have betrayed all our people if you had been Nazi spies."

Isak rushed into explanation of his own. "The Gestapo's methods are frighteningly efficient. To survive, we must be careful. We in the underground don't even know who our leaders are. If we break under torture, we can betray only a handful of our people. Forgive me. It had to be done."

Spock was eyeing Daras. "I do not understand," he said. "You are a Nazi. A 'Hero of the Fatherland.' We saw you decorated."

"I'm an Ekosian . . . fighting the terrible thing that's happened to my people. The decoration was for betraying my own father to the Party."

At Kirk's look of revulsion, she added hastily, "My father's idea. He was very close to the Führer; but when he saw the change, where it was leading, he turned against the Party. He was imprisoned. Melakon sentenced him to death."

"Melakon?" Kirk said.

Abrom explained. "The Deputy Führer. He's taken over."

Daras spoke to Kirk. "My father denounced me, making it seem I had betrayed him. It gave me a weapon to continue the fight."

Spock was still trying to reconcile her story with facts as he knew them. "But how could that have seemed right to John Gill?"

"Who?" Abrom said.

"The Führer," Kirk said. "He's one of our people."

"What people is that?" Abrom asked.

Kirk hesitated a moment. "I'm Captain James Kirk of the United Space Ship *Enterprise*. This is my First Officer, Mr. Spock. John Gill, your Führer, was sent here as a cultural observer by the Federation."

The statement stunned Daras. "The Führer is . . . is an alien?"

"That is correct," Spock said.

The girl's face was incredulous. "I grew up to admire him. Later, to hate, despise everything he stands for. But I always believed he was one of us. To learn he's an alien sent to destroy us—"

"That was not his mission—ever," Kirk said. "It was to report, not to interfere. Something went wrong. That's what we're here to find out. And to correct. We must see him."

"Impossible!" Isak exclaimed. "Even if this were some other time, it would be impossible. He sees no one, permits no one but Melakon to see him. He is under maximum security."

Kirk and Spock exchanged a look. "Under maximum security. Is he so afraid?" Kirk said.

Isak's fists had clenched. "There are many of us—Ekosians and younger Zeons—who would gladly give our lives to kill him!"

Kirk turned to him. "I can't explain what's happened. This is against every principle John Gill believed in. But our only chance is to see him—quickly."

"That's impossible now," Daras said shortly. "He makes a speech tonight from the Chancellery. The top Party officials will be there."

"Will *you* be there?" Kirk said.

"Of course." She added bitterly, "As the symbol of the proper attitude toward the Fatherland."

Spock spoke to Kirk. "As an honored member of the Party, she should be able to get us past the guards."

Daras protested. "Only a few of the top, most trusted Party members will be allowed into the Chancellery. The nation will watch on the viewscreens."

"You'll have to get us in there," Kirk said.

"Into the Chancellery? It would be suicide, Captain Kirk."

Isak turned to her. "It's a risk to live at all, the way things are going. If the Captain thinks he has a chance, I'm willing to commit suicide with him."

Daras whirled on him. "You? A Zeon? You expect to get into the Chancellery too?"

"It's my fight even more than yours!"

"If you'll risk it, Daras," Kirk said, "I have an idea that just might work."

It was a challenge she had to meet.

They had commandeered a command car. And Gestapo uniforms. Spock and Isak were helmeted as troopers, but Kirk, carrying a camera, wore a Captain's insignia. The other two held lights.

As Kirk saw the guards at the Chancellery entrance, he lifted the camera to conceal his face, saying, "Turn on the lights."

The guards squinted angrily in the sudden glare. One said, "You. What is your business here?"

The second command car pulled up at the curb, and as Daras got out of it, Kirk, Spock and Isak gathered around her, photographing her. She smiled, waving for the camera, then mounted the steps. Still shooting, still flaring the lights, the three fell into line behind her. The guards had recognized her. Passing them, she said, "The Führer's special documentary corps. The door, please, Corporal. And smile at me as I enter it."

Dazzled but smiling, the guard opened the door.

The party moved forward into a corridor. Daras was trembling. Spock lowered his voice. "You know, Captain, I begin to sense what you Earthmen enjoy in gambling. However carefully one computes the odds of success, there is a certain exhilaration in the risk."

"We may make a human of you yet, Mr. Spock—if we live long enough."

The open doors of the audience chamber, holding a collection of Party officials, were directly ahead of them.

Kirk spoke to Daras. "Where does the Führer enter?"

"He doesn't. They watch him on that big screen. He broadcasts from the end of the room where the two guards are. For security."

Kirk saw a window at the end of the room, draped and flanked by the two guards.

"Where's the entrance?" Kirk said.

"It's heavily guarded, Captain."

"Where?" he said again.

"Straight down the corridor."

Kirk was getting his bearings. The guards were armed with submachine guns. They were standing on either side of a door. One of them peered through a small window set into the door.

"You're not going to try to get into the broadcast room?" Daras whispered.

"We're going to look," Kirk told her.

Isak spoke. "Distract the guard long enough for me to get the machine gun. The broadcasting room is a small booth. I could shoot through the door."

Kirk turned quickly, his voice hard. "You're not here for your personal satisfaction. We need Gill and we need him alive. Is that clear?"

Isak finally nodded resignedly. He moved forward with them and a guard, gun raised, stepped toward them. Kirk was abruptly full of business as a documentary cameraman.

"Hold it there," he told the guard. "This is for the record of the Führer's Final Solution speech. The behind-the-scenes story."

"We want to photograph the men responsible for the Führer's safety," Isak said. "The men who make the Führer's decisions possible."

Daras's presence with the trio reassured the man. He returned to the door and, standing at attention, turned his best profile for the camera. Kirk spoke to the other guard. "You. Over there. I want you together, guns held at the ready."

They moved away from the door, and Kirk positioned them so that Spock could look through its tiny window. He spotted Gill sitting at a table, facing a TV camera. He nodded to Kirk. The guards moved back and Kirk said, "Thank you. There'll be more coverage later."

Spock had rejoined Kirk. "It *is* John Gill. But he did not move, did not once look up, Captain."

"That might be part of the plan—the semi-divine detachment."

"Or a deep psychosis," Spock said.

"It might be even simpler. He could be drugged. We need McCoy, Mr. Spock." He turned to Daras. "Is there a place we can be alone for a few minutes? I'm going to send for help. There's no time to explain. A closet—any place will do."

"The cloakroom," Isak suggested.

Alone with Kirk, Spock made last adjustments on the communicator. He flipped it open. "Spock to *Enterprise*. Come in, *Enterprise . . .*"

On the Starship, reception was bad. Uhura made hasty moves with her switches. *"Enterprise,* Lieutenant Uhura."

Kirk took the communicator. "This is the Captain. Put Dr. McCoy on."

"Yes, sir. We don't read you well. You're nine points into the low frequency band."

"We've had some difficulty, Lieutenant. Patch historical computer into ship's uniform section. I want

22

McCoy outfitted as a Gestapo doctor, Nazi Germany, old Earth date 1944. Make him a colonel."

"Yes, sir. Dr. McCoy coming on."

"McCoy here, Captain."

"Bones, we need you. Have Transporter lock on these coordinates."

"What have you got, Jim?"

"We've found John Gill. At least, we've seen him. He may be drugged or hypnotized or psychotic. You'll have to make a determination. Hurry with that uniform."

Daras opened the cloakroom door, her face ashen. "Isak just heard two security men talking. They picked up your broadcast and pinpointed it within this building. They're starting a search."

Spock closed the cloakroom door. "If there's a delay in transporting Dr. McCoy, I suggest we cancel the plan."

Kirk spoke again into the communicator. "Kirk to *Enterprise*. What's happening?"

"The Doctor is in the Transporter, sir. He's having trouble with the uniform."

"Send him down naked if you have to. Kirk out."

But the shimmer had appeared near a corner of the cloakroom. Daras fell back, her face blank with amazement as the sparkles materialized into McCoy. He held the uniform's coat over an arm and was clutching a boot.

"It's . . . true," Daras whispered. "I only half-believed the things you said. But this—it's magnificent."

McCoy sat down on a bench, trying to pull on the boot. "Stupid computer made a mistake in the measurements. The right boot's too tight." He jerked at it angrily.

"Doctor, there's a logical way to proceed," Spock said. "Point your toe, pull with a steady, unemotional pressure on either side of the boot. We have no time to waste on emotionalism."

McCoy gave him a sour glance but obeyed. The boot

23

went on. "This is Dr. McCoy, our Chief Medical Officer," Spock told Daras. "Doctor, Daras, secretary of the National Socialist Party."

Shouldering into the coat, McCoy said, "How do you do? Now what's this about John Gill, Jim?"

The door was kicked open. A grim-faced Eneg, followed by two troopers, submachine guns leveled, walked into the room.

They had all tensed, waiting for immediate death. When it didn't come, Daras fumbled for a cover story. "Chairman Eneg—" she nodded at McCoy "—the Colonel . . . has had too much to drink."

"I see," Eneg said.

Kirk and Spock had averted their faces lest the Party Chairman recognize them. Kirk, his face still turned, said, "We were afraid he would embarrass the Führer."

"A doctor should have more pride," Daras said.

Eneg nodded. "You were right to conceal him. There is a spy in this building with a secret transmitter. We're conducting a search. Hail the Führer!"

After a startled pause, Kirk, Spock and Daras snapped a salute in reply. Eneg left and a trooper pulled the door shut behind them. Kirk drew a deep breath, and Spock said, "I do not understand how he could have failed to recognize us."

"This is our lucky day. Luck, Mr. Spock, is something you refuse to recognize."

"I shall reconsider, Captain."

Out in the corridor, a buzzer sounded. "It's the Führer's speech," Daras said quickly.

"Let's go," Kirk said.

They followed her out of the cloakroom, down the corridor and into the main room. Isak saw them come in and nodded, relieved. The TV screen imaged a Nazi banner, then cut quickly to a close shot of the Führer. There was a general shout of "Hail the Führer!" Kirk, Spock and McCoy mouthed the slogan. The TV camera angle had been planned for drama, leaving the

24

screened face half-shadowed. The voice coming from the speaker was calm, reasoned.

"Ekosians, the job ahead is difficult. It requires courage and dedication. It requires faith."

Wild applause broke out. The voice went on. "The Zeon colony has existed for nearly half a century . . ."

"Watch the mouth," Kirk whispered to McCoy.

But the camera had switched to a low shot in which the table's microphone hid the lower portion of the Führer's face.

"If we fulfill our own greatness, that will all be ended." Excited cheers broke into the voice. When they ended, the voice said, "Working together we can find a solution."

Spock leaned to Kirk. "The speech does not follow any logical pattern, Captain."

"Just random sentences strung together."

"He looks drugged, Jim, at an almost cataleptic stage," McCoy said.

The voice was back. "What we do may sometimes be difficult, but it is necessary if we are to reach our goal. And we will reach that goal."

McCoy had straightened in his seat. "We've got to get close to him."

Daras stared at him. Then she rose, starting to edge her way through the crowd toward the door. Isak joined them, helping to clear a path. A few annoyed faces turned, then broke into smiles as Daras was recognized. As the others followed her, the irritation came back, but McCoy's Gestapo uniform aroused respect. They made the corridor.

They could hear the voice continuing the speech.

"Every action we take must be decisive. Every thought directed toward a goal. This planet can become a paradise if we are willing to pay the price . . ."

At the windowed door of the broadcast booth, the guards were listening to their Führer's voice, but their machine guns were still leveled. Isak held the lights as Kirk arranged his camera. "I want a picture of you two with the Hero of the Fatherland as you all listen to the Führer's stirring words." He turned to Daras. "There, stand between them."

The flattered men made room for her while the voice said, "As each cell of the body works in discipline and harmony for the good of the entire being . . ."

Kirk, lining up the shot through his camera, nodded, and McCoy chopped a guard across the neck. Spock neck-pinched the second one. Both dropped. Spock tried the door and found it locked.

". . . so must each of you work to make our dream a reality—to find a lasting solution. Long live Ekos. Long live our Party!"

A storm of cheers greeted John Gill's final words. Kirk and McCoy, searching the guards' pockets, came up with a key. It opened the booth's door. As the group entered, the Führer didn't move. Kirk and Isak dragged in the guards. Over their heads, a wall monitor showed Melakon standing at the main room's podium. He gestured for silence. "The Führer has given us our orders. And we pledge him our lives in the sacred task. Death to Zeon!"

"Death to Zeon!" the crowd shouted.

McCoy straightened from examining Gill. "Definitely drugged. Almost comatose."

"What drug?" Spock said.

"I can't identify it without a medi-comp. And without knowing, giving an antidote could be dangerous."

"Is there anything you can do, Bones?"

"A general stimulant, but it's risky."

As Kirk said, "Take the risk," Melakon was speaking from the monitor.

"For years we have been defiled by the Zeon presence on our planet. We've tried many solutions to the Zeon problem—limiting them to separate areas of our cities, confining them. But despite our best efforts, they remain like a cancer, eating away at our state . . ."

McCoy gave Gill a hypo injection. Watching, Isak said, "There's no reaction. Whatever you gave him, it isn't working."

While McCoy used his scanner, Melakon was saying, "Like a disease, the Zeons appear from every side. You smash one, and two more turn up. Ten minutes ago, on our Führer's orders, our troops began their historic mission. In our cities, the elimination has started. Within an hour, the Zeon blight will be forever removed from the face of Ekos."

Kirk leaned over Gill. "Can you increase the dosage?"

"I'm working in the dark, Jim. I could kill him."

Daras said, "If they find us here, we'll all be killed."

At Kirk's nod, McCoy used the hypo again.

Daras turned to Isak. "It's begun. It's finally begun." She had covered her face with her hands when McCoy looked up at Kirk. "The stimulant's working. He's near the level of consciousness." He lifted one of Gill's eyelids. "As though he's in a light sleep. That's as much as I dare do."

"Spock, see if you can get through to him by the mind probe. If you can't, Bones will have to use a heavier dose, no matter what it does."

There was a roar from the monitor. Old-fashioned rockets were taking off from launching pads; and Melakon's voice said, "Our space fleet is now on its way toward Zeon, both manned and unmanned weapons. This is the time of destiny! Hail the Führer!" There was a pause. "Hail Victory, Ekosians!"

Daras went to Kirk. "There's one chance left. With the weapons you have, you could destroy the fleet!"

Kirk shook his head. "That would mean the death of thousands of Ekosian spacemen."

The crowd was chanting from the monitor, "Hail Victory! Hail Victory!"

Daras cried, "But against those thousands are millions upon millions of innocent Zeon lives! We must choose the lesser of two evils, Captain!"

"We could save Zeon that way, Daras—but not Ekos."

Spock had completed his mind probe. "Captain, in

his condition, Gill cannot *initiate* speech or any other function. But he can reply to direct questions."

Kirk looked at his one-time teacher. "They've kept what's left of him as a figurehead."

"Exactly, Captain. The real power, for these last years, has been Melakon."

"Turn that monitor speaker down," Kirk told Daras. As quiet filled the room, he went to Gill, bending over the table. "Gill, why did you abandon your mission? Why did you interfere in this culture?"

The face was expressionless and the voice barely audible. "Planet . . . fragmented . . . divided. Took lesson . . . from Earth history . . ."

"Why Nazi Germany?" Kirk said. "I took that history course from you. You knew what the Nazis were like!"

"Most . . . efficient state . . . Earth . . . ever knew . . ."

Spock spoke. "True, Captain. That tiny country, divided, beaten, bankrupt, rose in a few years to stand only one step from global domination."

"It was brutal, perverted! It had to be destroyed at a terrible cost! Why pick that example?"

"Perhaps Gill felt that such a state, run benignly, could accomplish efficiency without sadism."

"Worked," Gill said. "At first . . . it worked. Then Melakon began . . . takeover, used the . . . gave me the drug . . ."

He fell silent.

"Gill! Gill, can you hear me? You'll have to tell these people what happened. You're the only one who can stop the slaughter!"

Gill slumped. McCoy, running his scanner over him, shook his head. "He's still alive, but the drug they use is too strong."

"Give him another shot," Kirk said.

Daras turned from the door, crying, "Guards!"

"Bones, we're out of time—"

SS men were running to the broadcast booth, Eneg

behind them. Kirk issued orders hard and fast. "Spock, take off that helmet! Daras, draw your gun! You, too, McCoy and Isak! Draw your guns! Point them at Spock!"

The guards rushed in. Behind them Eneg took in the spectacle of the three guns trained at Spock's head. Kirk indicated Daras. "She's just captured a Zeon spy who was attempting to assassinate the Führer. We'll make a present of him to Melakon."

The guards grabbed Spock, and Isak spoke quickly to Eneg. "Chairman, we *must* take this spy to Melakon!"

Eneg was looking at their faces, one by one. Finally, he turned to the guards. "Pass them on my responsibility." He left, and Isak, whispering to Daras, said, "I wasn't allowed to tell you. Eneg is with us." He spoke to a guard. "You heard the Chairman. Bring the spy along." The two guards stood aside while he, Daras and McCoy took Spock outside the broadcast booth and into the corridor. Kirk hung back, his eyes on the hypo that still lay on the table.

Melakon was surrounded by congratulating admirers. The guards moved in to push Spock through the throng.

"What's this?" Melakon demanded.

Isak answered. "A spy, Excellency."

"A rare prize." Daras had stepped forward. "The Deputy Führer can see this is no ordinary Zeon."

In the broadcast booth, Kirk finished injecting more hypo stimulant into Gill's arm. "Professor Gill, can you hear me now? You've got to speak. This is our last chance. Please come out of it!"

Melakon was interested in the spy. He had seized Spock's chin, turning it to examine his profile. "Not a Zeon. Definitely not."

"The Deputy Führer," Daras said, "is an authority on the genetics of racial purity. How would he classify this specimen?"

"Difficult. A very difficult question from such a

charming questioner." He returned to his study of Spock, pleased to parade his knowledge. "Note those sinister eyes, the malformed ears. Definitely an inferior race."

Kirk was struggling to get Gill on his feet. "You're the only one who can stop them! You've *got* to speak!"

Under his glazed eyes, Gill opened his mouth. Then he slumped again.

Melakon meanwhile was discovering other stigmata of racial inferiority in Spock. "Note the low forehead, denoting stupidity. The dull look of a trapped animal . . ."

Spock's right eyebrow lifted; and Melakon spoke to the guard. "You may take him now for interrogation. But I want the body saved for the cultural museum. He'll make an interesting display."

There was a stir in the crowd. A startled murmur grew. Melakon turned toward the podium. Gill had appeared on the screen. He was swaying, staring dazedly at nothing. After one horrified look, Melakon spoke to one of Spock's guards.

"Go to the booth. See to the Führer at once. He is ill. Turn off that camera in there!"

Gill opened his mouth. "People . . . of Ekos. Hear me . . ."

Melakon whirled to the audience. "The Führer is ill. The strain of the day has been too much!"

Gill, Kirk in the shadows behind him, fought to go on. Melakon's voice came over the speaker in the broadcast booth. "I suggest we all leave the hall. Let our Führer rest!"

Kirk saw the handle of the booth door turn. The door was locked, but the guard outside began to pound on it. Gill's voice was stronger. "People of Ekos. We've been betrayed by a self-seeking adventurer who has led us all to the brink of disaster. To Zeon, I swear this was not aggression by the Ekosian people . . ."

The guard ran back to whisper in Melakon's ear; and Gill said, ". . . only of one evil man. Melakon is a traitor to his own people and to all that we stand for . . ."

Melakon grabbed the guard's machine gun and, swinging around, leveled it at the booth curtain.

"To the Zeon people," Gill was saying, "I pledge reparation and goodwill."

Melakon sprayed a lethal hail of lead into the curtain. The crowd was silent, stunned. The booth window shattered as Kirk dived forward, dragging Gill to the floor.

Melakon continued to fire into the booth. Isak drew his pistol and pulled the trigger. Melakon jerked forward under the shot's impact, tried to train his gun on Isak—and collapsed. An SS Colonel snatched the weapon from his hands and pointed it at Isak.

"Hold it, Colonel!"

It was Eneg. "There has been enough killing." The Colonel hesitated and Eneg said, "Now we'll start to live the way the Führer intended us to live!"

The Colonel dropped the gun.

Gill's eyes were clear, but the breast of his uniform was crimson. As Kirk cradled his head in his arms, a tiny trickle of blood flowed from his mouth. He looked up at Kirk, recognizing him. "I was wrong," he whispered. "The non-interference directive is the only way. We must stop the slaughter . . ."

"You did that, Professor. You told them in time."

"Even historians fail to learn from history—repeat the same mistakes. Let the killing end, Kirk. Let—"

He choked on a bloody sob and crumpled in Kirk's arms.

"Professor. . . ?"

He looked up at the sound of Spock's voice. "Captain, are you all right?"

"Yes, Mr. Spock."

He lowered Gill to the floor, got up and unlocked the door.

Eneg was standing beside Spock. Behind them, Mc-Coy, Daras and Isak waited, their faces solemn as though they knew what he had to tell them.

"He's dead."

There was a long stillness before Isak said, "For so long I've prayed to hear that. Now I'm sorry."

"So was he," Kirk said.

Isak moved to him. "You have given the rest of us a new chance."

"I thank you too," Eneg said. "But go now. We must do the rest."

"Eneg and I," Daras said, "will go on the air now ... offer a plan to our people ... for all our people— Ekosians and Zeons alike."

As Eneg followed her into the broadcast booth, he turned to say, "It is time to stop the bloodshed—to bury our dead."

"Mr. Spock," Kirk said, "I think the planet is in good hands."

"Indeed, Captain. With a union of two cultures, this system would make a fine addition to the Federation."

Kirk opened his communicator. "Kirk to *Enterprise*."

"*Enterprise* here, Captain."

"Beam us aboard, Lieutenant Uhura."

Their Ekosian experience still mystified Spock. He left his bridge station to go to Kirk. "I will never understand humans, Captain. How could a man as brilliant, a mind as logical as John Gill's have made such a fatal mistake?"

"He drew a wrong conclusion from history. The trouble with the Nazis wasn't simply that their leaders were evil and psychotic men. They were. But the real trouble was the leader principle."

McCoy had joined them. "A man who holds that much power, Spock, even with the best intentions, can't resist the urge to play God."

"I was able to gather the meaning, Doctor," Spock said.

"There's an old Earth saying," Kirk said, "that

everything happens for the best. John Gill found Ekos divided. He leaves it unified."

"That also proves another Earth saying, Spock. Absolute power corrupts absolutely. Damn clever, these Earthmen, wouldn't you say?"

Spock turned to McCoy. "Earthmen such as Rameses, Alexander, Caesar, Napoleon, Hitler, Lee Kuan. Your whole history is Man seeking absolute power."

"Now just a minute, Spock—"

Kirk looked at them. "Gentlemen," he said, "we've just been through one civil war. Let's not start another."

THE GAMESTERS OF TRISKELION
(Margaret Armen)

Gamma II was a planet so small it scarcely merited the name. Reportedly uninhabited, it nevertheless boasted automatic communications and astrogation installations. Making a routine check of these stations was Kirk's motive for ordering Uhura and Chekov to beam down with him to the surface.

At Chekov's announcement that the *Enterprise* was now circling Gamma II in standard orbit, Kirk nodded.

"Very good, Mr. Chekov. Lieutenant Uhura?"

"Ready, sir."

"Then let's go." And turning to Spock, added, "Commander, you mind the store."

"Yes, Captain."

His Science Officer, moving swiftly to the vacated command chair, watched them enter the bridge elevator. From here on, he thought, it would be the old story—the Transporter room, the "Energize" command and then the sparkled glitter of their dematerialization.

But for once it was a new story. Though Kirk, Uhura and Chekov took their places on the platform, and despite Scott's push at his second switch, they did not shimmer out in the orthodox Transporter effect. One moment they were where they should be, and the next, they were simply and bafflingly gone.

The startled Scott jerked back his first switch. Then more alarmed than he cared to admit to himself, he gave himself to a frantic spinning of dials. If he'd hoped for their reappearance on the platform, there was none. Yet more alarmed, he hit his bridge communicator to say into it, "Scott to bridge."

"Spock here, Mr. Scott."

"Mr. Spock—the Captain, Lieutenant Uhura and Mr. Chekov—they did not dematerialize. They just disappeared. They took their positions on the platform—and then they simply went. Where, sir?"

"I presume you mean in a manner inconsistent with the usual workings of the Transporter."

Under the pressure of his anxiety, Scott's blood pressure rose. "Of course I mean that! Do you think I'd call you if they had just beamed down?"

The tranquil voice said, "Have you reversed your controls, Mr. Scott?"

"I've made all the proper checks. There was nothing—nothing. No light flashes . . . no outlinings of shimmer-out. Nothing. They're just gone, sir, and I can't bring them back."

"Power surges?

"Not from here, sir. The dials are right, and the Transporter functioned perfectly."

"Recheck your equipment, Mr. Scott. I'll scan for them on the planet's surface."

Meanwhile, on that surface of Gamma II, the materialization of the *Enterprise* trio was as out of order as their departure from the Starship. Instead of duplicating the erect positions they had assumed on the Transporter platform, they fell flat on their faces until, in an uncontrollable roll, they were brought up against the foot of a jagged rock formation towering steep to a red and greenish sky. Kirk was the first to regain his feet. Dizzy, shaking his head against the vertigo, he half-realized that they had landed in a most peculiar place—a paved area marked by random lines that delineated triangles, rectangles, hexagons, rhomboids—a hodgepodge of every conceivable geometrical design.

Chekov, stirring, struggled up, staring around him. No rhetorician, he said, "What happened, sir?"

"Must have been a Transporter malfunction."

"A rough trip, Captain."

Going to the still prone Uhura, Kirk pulled her to her feet. Puzzledly.

"This isn't Gamma II," he told them. "Look at the color of that sky."

Clutching his arm for support, Uhura said, "This is the craziest landing pad I've ever seen."

She spoke truth. It *was* a mad landing pad: an area about the size of a tennis court but otherwise bearing no resemblance to one. There was no coherent pattern whatever to the conglomeration of demented geometry around them. Helter-skelter to no obvious point, it proliferated itself meaninglessly. However, a closer scrutiny of it suggested that they were standing in what could only have been a playing board created by lunatics for some equally lunatic game.

Kirk, careful to shade his eyes, stared up again at the sinister sky.

"That's a trinary sun up there," he said.

"Then you're right, sir, and we're not on Gamma II," Chekov said. "And if we're not, where are we?"

Kirk managed a wry grin. "I'd like to know that answer too, Mr. Chekov." And unbelted his communicator, flipped it open to say, "Kirk to *Enterprise*."

But intuition had already warned him that the Starship would fail to respond. Nor would the communicators of the others function.

"Dead, sir," Chekov said unnecessarily.

He was rebelting his device when Uhura, pointing to the cliff base, whispered an urgent, "Captain!"

Following the line of her outstretched forefinger, Kirk said, "No, this is not Gamma II. That's an uninhabited planetoid. This one clearly is. We appear to have company, friends."

Close under the shadow of the escarpment, four creatures were standing, observant and intrigued by the strangers' appearance, but their postures hostile, alert. Outstanding in physique was a huge blond male, a Viking who might have been resurrected from some

Norse saga's Valhalla. Beside him, squat but thickly muscled as an ape, was Neanderthal Man himself, his low brow shock-haired almost to the nose. And next to him was a female whom some unknown deity had endowed with a bush of yellowish, black-spotted hair, leopardlike. Two fangs protruding from her upper teeth hung over her lower lip. The fangs were pointed.

But the fourth being was the true astonishment—a gorgeous Amazon of a bronze-haired girl, the sapphire of her dark-lashed eyes flashing with the general hostility. But like the rest of her companions, she wore a metallic collar around her lovely neck, inset with some glittering gem under the ear.

Both women carried daggers in the clumsy belts that confined their smockish coarse garments at the waist. Moreover, they had additional weapons, the males equipped with staves ending in blades at one end and grapples at the other.

Wordlessly, the alien group moved forward until they had spaced themselves evenly around the triangle enclosing Kirk, Chekov and Uhura.

The giant Viking finally spoke.

"I am Lars," he said. "He is Kloog. She of the beast's hair is Tamoon. The other she is Shahna."

Fierce suspicion deepened the deep voice. Where usually Kirk would have met such an introduction with one of his own, he decided that this was no time for an exchange of courtesies. So, instead, he said quietly, "Phasers at stun." And added, "Just in case."

The case arose.

Lars, jaw set, stepped forward and, extending a formidable arm, attempted to wrench Chekov's phaser from him. Kirk promptly fired his. Nothing . . . nothing. And when he ordered phaser action from Chekov and Uhura, the nothing was repeated. Swiftly, the *Enterprise* Captain made an adjustment on his weapon and once more tried to activate it. It was as dead as the communicators. Then hurling the useless phaser at the still oncoming blond giant, he ducked sideways to get to the rear of his adversary. Behind him, he was aware that the other three aliens had already subdued Chekov and Uhura, and, with an heroic effort, controlled his ingrained sense of responsibility for them to leap on Lars's heavy-muscled back. He managed a neck chop. It stunned Lars. The giant didn't drop, but he stumbled, reeling, dazed, too shocked for instant reaction.

Seizing advantage of the temporary respite, Kirk added several other telling blows to the vulnerable join of neck to backbone. The last one doubled up the redoubtable Siegfried. And straightening in satisfaction, Kirk turned to his less fortunate shipmates.

It was the beautiful Shahna who had downed Uhura with Tamoon's assistance. But now she left the leopard-haired creature to guard Uhura in order to concentrate her own belligerent and very dangerous attention on Kirk.

His moment of self-satisfaction had been expensive. Too slowly he realized that Shahna was hurtling toward him, and, jumping back, was barely able to dodge the vicious slash of her spear. But the cliff wall blocked all further retreat. Shahna snatched the dagger from the belt that held her shoulder harness in place and, flying at him, pushed its point painfully against the skin of his throat. He looked away from the sapphire eyes so full of triumphant hate, saying to himself, "Okay. Maybe this is it."

To their rear, Tamoon and Kloog had jerked his two companions erect, and Lars rose slowly to his feet, still groggy from the neck chops. As to Kirk, he was now half-crouched against the cliff's rock face, immobilized lest the infuriated Shahna drive the dagger through to his backbone. He gasped, choking, and to his relieved but immense surprise, the pressure eased slightly. Instantly, he came out of his crouch, and at the same moment, a new figure abruptly appeared in the center triangle.

"Hold!" it cried.

At once Shahna lowered her dagger. Ignoring her,

38

the stranger spoke directly to Kirk. "Excellent, Captain Kirk!"

There'd been no excellence about it—just an instinctive use of Space Academy training. But there was no time for reminiscence on the stiff courses through which the Academy put its cadets, for the masterful newcomer was leaving the triangle for a closer approach to the *Enterprise* people. Was it his dress which conveyed the impression of undisputed authority? Perhaps. For he wore no smock but a togalike garment, its shoulder bearing a gold-embroidered emblem; nor did he carry any weapons. Yet the unarmed stranger also wore a gemmed, metallic collar under his expressionless features, a face Kirk judged to be in its middle thirties.

He spoke again.

"Although we expected strength and competitive spirit, Captain Kirk, we are greatly pleased."

Kirk was silent, too angry to trust himself to speak. Kloog was dragging a squirming Chekov toward them, followed by Lars who clutched a struggling, kicking Uhura over his big shoulder. Thrust into positions near Kirk, their two captors divested them of phasers, tricorders and communicators.

Kirk spoke to his people. "Either of you hurt?"

The shaken Uhura shook her head. "I—I don't think so, sir." But the wildly furious Chekov yelled, "No, nobody's hurt—*yet*, Captain!"

"Admirable, Chekov," observed the black-robed man. "Admirable! You also, Uhura. I can see you will all prove invaluable here."

Once more Chekov yelled. "Who is he, sir?"

"I am Galt," he was told. "I am the Master Thrall of the planet Triskelion. I have been sent to welcome you."

A highly undesirable welcome. Even as Galt was speaking, Kirk felt unseen hands at his neck as they fitted one of the jeweled collars around it. He pushed at them, but they were intangible; nor would any exertion budge the lock. He accepted the inevitable, trying to relax until he saw that the same invisible fingers had attached the collar to a chain they affixed to the rock wall. To his right, and visibly, Shahna, Lars and Tamoon were busy shackling his crewmates to chained collars.

"Now," Galt said, "you are prepared for your training."

For the first time Kirk addressed him. "How do you know our names?"

"The Providers were expecting you, Captain. They arranged your ... transfer here."

So it had not been a Transporter malfunction that had sent them tumbling onto the wrong planet. Their arrival was the consequence of interference, an interference as powerful as it was inexplicable.

He waited a moment before he said, "These Providers of yours. Are they—?"

Galt's interruption was sharp. "Correction, Captain! The Providers are not *ours*. We are *theirs*."

A slave state.

"And what do the Providers want with us?"

"You are to be trained, of course. What other use is there for Thralls?"

"Thralls? I think there's been a mistake. We're officers of a United Space Ship bound on Federation business."

"There's been no mistake. Your old titles mean nothing here. You are Thralls now. And to be taken to the training enclosure. Come, places have already been prepared for you."

"We will do nothing until we get a satisfactory explanation of this outrage. Who are you? What is this place? And what do you think you're going to do with us?"

"I have told you. This place is the planet Triskelion. You will be trained and spend the rest of your lives here. Don't trouble yourself with thoughts of escape. It is impossible. No Thrall leaves Triskelion. Lars, unchain them from the rock."

As the heavy links were removed, Galt added, "Now you are able to accompany me to your quarters." He hesitated. Then, persuasively, he said, "Captain, no harm is intended you."

Kirk looked at the four subservient Thralls as they marshaled Chekov and Uhura before them. Then, shrugging, he followed their Master's lead.

McCoy, on the *Enterprise* bridge, had joined Spock at his scanner, noting that an Ensign Jana Haines had been assigned to the absent Chekov's console, another junior officer at Uhura's position. Scott, emerging from the elevator, stalked over to the two at the scanner.

"Mr. Spock, I've checked the Transporter from one end to the other. Every circuit is perfect. Whatever that power surge was, it didn't come from the Transporter or any other system on this ship!"

"I'm beginning to believe that, Mr. Scott. I have conducted two sweeps of the planet's surface. There is no sign of life."

McCoy reddened. "Well, what the devil's happened then? Does that mean that their atoms are still floating around out there?"

"No, Doctor. Even that would show up on the sensors."

"Then where are they?" Scott shouted.

Mild as ever, Spock said, "The only answers are negative, Mr. Scott. No magnetic storms, no ionic interference and, as you say, no breakdown in your equipment."

It was McCoy's turn to shout. "A negative attitude isn't much good to us, Spock! We just can't leave them out there—" He broke off to add a desperate "—wherever they are."

"We shall continue sensor scans, Doctor. At the moment, that is all we can do except hope for a rational explanation."

"Hope!" McCoy jeered. "I thought that was a strictly human failing. Vulcans don't indulge it!"

"Prolonged exposure to the failing results in a certain amount of contamination, Doctor." And turning away, Spock resumed operation of his scanner.

A corridor giving on to a row of box stalls was the destination of the *Enterprise* captives. Box stalls, their doors centrally cut, the upper half barred, the lower one locked. Herded down the corridor, they were halted before three stalls, staring in unbelief at the nameplates fastened to the doors. They read: *Kirk, Chekov, Uhura.*

Kirk had been up against such assured, though alien, intelligence on his mission "to go where no man had gone before." For a long moment, he was astounded by this Triskelion variety. Then, once again, he shrugged. Now there could be no answer to the arrogant certainty of the beings Galt called "The Providers." But tomorrow was another day. And Spock on the *Enterprise* would be overworking his own not inconsiderable intelligence to apply his equally efficient equipment to discovery of the answer.

Beside him, Galt said, "These are your quarters. Open, Shahna."

Obediently, she removed a small disk from her harness, placing it on the three locks of the cells. While she was working on the third, Kirk shot Chekov a quick, significant look to which his navigator nodded.

The three doors open, Galt said, "Enter."

Kirk and Chekov took two apparently compliant steps only to whirl, whirl and lunge at their nearest jailer. Kirk struck Kloog in the midriff with all the power of his powerful shoulders, knocking Neanderthal Man to his knees. Then, in his command voice, he shouted, "Lieutenant Uhura!"

She gathered herself, and, shoving Tamoon who was flanking her, sent the fanged one spinning against Lars. Then running to Kirk, he, she and Chekov raced down the corridor to the still open entrance.

Lacking eyes in the back of their heads, they couldn't see Galt close his, his face deeply concentrated. But they could feel the results. Suddenly, the jewels in their slave collars went into a sickening, greenish glow. The race ended as the collars tightened, their faces contorted in agony as the anguished choking continued, driving them to their knees, hands futilely clutching at the strangling collars. They sank down, unaware that Galt was watching them with clinical detachment. Unaware of anything but pain, they failed to see that Galt had once more shut his cold eyes in concentration.

As Kirk collapsed on his back, the veins of his neck protruding, the jewel on his collar winked out. But it had done its work. Eons seemed to pass before his tortured throat could swallow and breath returned to his lungs. Then yet more eons crept by before he could get to his knees and, using his weakened arms, thrust himself up to his feet. Chekov and Uhura, watching him, used his method to recover theirs.

"That was foolish, Captain," said Galt. "I warned you that escape is impossible. The collars of obedience have proved that to you."

He nodded toward Kirk's cell. Kirk, hesitating, recognized the futility of defiance and entered it. As his friends followed his example, the cell doors were slammed shut.

It was bad news from Spock. Straightening from his scanner, he said, "They are not within the confines of this solar system, Doctor."

"It's been nearly an hour. Can people live that long as disassembled atoms in a Transporter beam?"

"I've never heard of a study being done. But it would be a fascinating research."

"*Fascinating!* Those are our friends out there! If they're still alive, that is."

"Precisely."

"The odds aren't good, Spock."

"No. I should say they are—"

"Don't quote odds. And don't give me anymore of your dispassionate logic. Just find them. Keep looking."

"I would welcome a suggestion—even an emotional one—as to where to look."

"The first time you've ever asked me for anything, and it has to be on an occasion like this!"

Chekov, supporting himself against the bars of his cell, spoke to Kirk in the next one. "Captain, the *Enterprise*— They'll be trying to find us, won't they?"

Uhura, her voice hopeless, answered him. "They'll be trying. But where do they look? We're here and we don't know where it is."

"This system's star is a trinary," Kirk said. "And that limits it a bit. However, we're a long way from the *Enterprise*—if we're even in the same dimension."

Before the others could reply, Lars came down the corridor to stop before Uhura's door. "I am your Drill Thrall," he announced. "You may call me Lars."

As he spoke, Kirk saw him insert a rod into the catching hole in her cage.

"What do you want with her?" he said.

"That is not your concern. Your Drill Thrall will attend you presently." Then through the opened door, he pushed a covered receptacle at her. "Here is nourishment. Consume it quickly. The time is limited."

Uhura, at the look in his eyes, drew back. "What—what do you want?"

He was eyeing her brunette beauty with increasing appreciation. "I have been selected for you."

Then walking into her sparsely furnished cubicle, he closed its door. But though the uneasy Uhura backed away from him, he maintained his confident, slow approach to her, a suggestive grin exposing his strong, white teeth. When he reached out a huge hand to caress her neck, she kicked him, but he seized the leg and, pushing her down to the cell floor, muttered, "Stop it. I told you you are mine."

She bit his lip.

At the sounds from her stall, Kirk and Chekov peered anxiously through their bars, Kirk calling,

"Uhura! Uhura, can you hear me?" But the noise of struggle went on. *"Lieutenant Uhura! Answer me!"*

The only answer was the sound of a blow. Alarmed, frustrated, Kirk shouted again, his face pressed against his bars. Then his own cell door opened to Shahna outside it, unarmed now and carrying another covered container of food.

Kirk grabbed it, threw it to the floor, glaring at the girl.

"What's happening to Lieutenant Uhura?" he yelled.

She made no reply, and in the silence came a final resounding crash from Uhura's stall. Desperate, Kirk called again. "Uhura! Are you all right?"

Lars provided the reassurance. Backing out of the stall and wiping blood from his bitten lip, he staggered as he protested plaintively, "It is not allowed to refuse selection. It is not allowed."

He moved away down the corridor, confused by such unexpected resistence; and Uhura, breathless, disheveled, spoke from her cell door.

"Yes, sir," she said. "I'm fine. He's big—but he's stupid."

Chekov, embarrassed by his concern for her, whispered, "Lieutenant, what happened?"

Uhura's hearing was as keen as her physical fitness. Shooting him an irritated look, she said, *"Nothing!* You're stupid too!"

Half-smiling, Kirk turned to see Shahna stooping, her russet hair a tumble of curls on her lovely head, busily restoring the scattered dishes of his food container to their places in it. Then setting it on a cubed stand, she said, "Come. It is the Nourishment Interval."

On the *Enterprise* bridge, Ensign Haines had left Chekov's position for Spock's computer console. She studied it intently before straightening to address Spock in the command chair.

"Sir, I get a fluctuating energy reading from this hydrogen cloud."

With Scott and McCoy, he went to her to replace her at the scanner.

"It's faint, sir," she said, "but it consistently reads in excess of predictable energy levels."

Spock adjusted several dials before he spoke. "There seems to be an ionization trail. Most interesting." And rapidly punched another computer key.

"What would account for that?" McCoy asked.

"The very question I have just fed into the computer, Doctor." And after a moment, added, "The answer is, nothing is known to us to account for it."

Scott rose to the defense of his Transporter. "It lacks both the power and the range to be responsible for it."

"Plot a follow course, Ensign Haines," Spock ordered.

"Aye, sir." And returning to her navigation console, swung switches before she said, "Course plotted, Mr. Spock. 310 Mark 241."

"Now lay in the course, Ensign Haines."

McCoy's voice rose in anger. "You're going to leave here without them and go off on some wild-goose chase halfway across the galaxy just because you found a discrepancy in a hydrogen cloud? Spock, where's your head? They've been gone for more than two hours!"

Spock, eyes on his scanner, said, "I am pursuing the Captain, Lieutenant Uhura and Ensign Chekov, Doctor, not an aquatic fowl. This is the only lead we have had."

"Course laid in, Mr. Spock," Ensign Haines reported.

"Initiate," he told her. "Warp Factor Two."

All eyes, including his, swerved to the main viewing screen.

Chekov was having his troubles too. He had backed nervously toward a bench in his stall as the fanged Tamoon opened its door, carrying his covered container of food. For to his horror, he had read covetous admiration in the slanting yellow eyes of the leopard-haired woman.

Stammering, he managed to ask, "You—you have been selected for me?"

She uttered a sad little whine. "No. I am only your Drill Thrall. I have brought you nourishment." And placing the container on the bench near him, made an obvious attempt to sound seductive. "It is a nice name —Chee-koo."

"Chekov," he said.

Though the fangs prohibited clear enunciation, she tried, speaking slowly and carefully. "Chee-koof." And beaming happily at him, said, "It is a *very* nice name —so nice you may call me Tamoon."

Chekov ran a cold hand down his face. "Pleased— pleased to know you . . . uh . . . miss."

"You are a fine specimen. I like you better than the others."

Chekov had amply demonstrated his courage in confrontation with galactic foes, but the clumsy coquetry of this alien female terrified him. When she said, "I will instruct you well so my Provider will take you," he backed still farther away. "That's very nice of you, miss, but—"

He had reached the bench. It hit the back of his knees so that he sat down on it abruptly only to be followed by Tamoon who dropped down beside him, the fanged mouth opened in a coy smile.

"If my Provider is pleased, we may even be selected for each other."

A slight groan escaped him, and Tamoon, her hoarse voice sympathetic, said, "You are hungry, Chee-koof." And uncovering his dishes, added, "Eat, Chee-koof."

"Chekov," he said. "No, thank you, I am not hungry."

But Kirk was. As he wolfed the contents of his metal bowls, Shahna watched him approvingly. Finishing, he gave a satisfied sigh.

"Didn't realize I was so hungry. Whatever you call that, it was good."

"It is nourishment," she said. "We call it that." And gathering up the emptied bowls, replaced them neatly in their container, Kirk studying her contemplatively, very much aware of her slim beauty.

"Nourishment," he repeated. "Very practical. And what do you call this collar?"

The sapphire eyes stared at him. "It is the sign of our Provider. By the color of the jewels, it can be known who holds us. When you are vended, you will also have a colored jewel."

"Vended? You mean sold? Bought?"

Puzzled, she said, "When you are developed. The Provider who offers the most quatloos puts his color on us."

Kirk nodded. "My race has another name for that —the word 'slavery.'"

Clearly the information meant nothing to her. As she covered the food container, he said, "The collar of obedience. Is Galt the only one who can operate it?"

"It is only to warn and punish."

"How does he make it work?"

She stared again. "It is not permitted to talk of that."

He pointed to the container she held. "Are you—will you bring me all my nourishment?"

"Of course. I am your Drill Thrall. I will train you well."

"I'm sure of that." And rising from his bench, he said, "I must say I've never seen a top sergeant who looked like you."

"I don't understand. What does that mean?"

Leaning back against the wall, he said, "It means that you're a very beautiful woman."

She rose from her stoop, shaking her head in bewilderment. "What is beautiful?"

"Hasn't anyone ever told you that before?"

"No. What is it?"

"It's hard to explain . . . a lot of things . . . it's—" Then lifting the shining metal cover from the container in her hands, he got up, and holding it close to

48

her face, said, "Look into this. What you see is beautiful."

But her mirrored reflection seemed to merely increase her bafflement; and as her discomfort was genuine, Kirk, changing the subject, asked, "Where were you born, Shahna?"

"Born? I have been here always."

"Where are your parents? Your father and mother. Where are they?"

"She who bore me was killed in a free-style match."

"Free style!"

"Do not be anxious. You will learn all these things."

"And the others, Lars and the one who is Chekov's Drill Thrall, they weren't born here. Where did they come from?"

"It is not permitted—" and breaking off at the sudden shrill of a bell, immediately recovered her self-possession, all business again. "The exercise interval," she told him. And turning to a small cabinetlike projection in a corner, pressed a button on its door. A well-disguised panel slid aside; reaching past it, she removed a harness from it similar to the one she wore.

"This is your training harness. Put it on."

Spock, with Ensign Haines beside him, was working on his scanners, but the eyes of the other bridge people were fixed on the main viewing screen, their faces taut with anxiety.

McCoy moved impatiently. "This is ridiculous! There's nothing out there—nothing at all!"

Scott nodded his agreement. "We're certainly heading into an empty sector."

Spock looked up. "Projecting back along the path of ionization, the nearest system is M24 Alpha."

"But that must be two dozen light years from here!" Scott cried.

"Eleven point six three zero, Mr. Scott."

"Spock, are you suggesting that they have been transported over a distance of—?" And sputtering in angry protest, said, "You're out of your Vulcan mind, Spock!"

"I am suggesting nothing, Doctor. I am following the only logical course available to us."

McCoy was not calmed but began to stride nervously around the bridge stations.

"This is the staff," Shahna said. "It can defend or attack."

It looked as though it could, its one end sharpened to a cutting edge, the other one hooked. Like Chekov and Uhura, Kirk said nothing, aware, however, that Lars and Tamoon were standing nearby on one of the gaming board shapes.

"I demonstrate," Shahna announced. "Lars."

As Lars moved toward her, holding a staff of his own, she spoke to the three strangers. "I shall attack. An attacker may use only the dark areas of the board, the defender only the light areas."

Positioned on the gaming board, the two instructors went through a brief show of quarterstaff technique, of expert lunging and pike work. Then Shahna said, "We stop now. Your Drill Thralls will begin your training."

"Hold!"

It was Galt's cold voice. By a means none of the *Enterprise* officers could detect, the Master Thrall had suddenly popped into the central triangle, another Thrall, hands manacled, beside him.

Galt was pleased to explain. "This one was slow to obey a command. For his punishment, he will be target Thrall." And ignoring the shock on the trainees' faces, said, "You will charge from here, striking the target Thrall as you pass. Uhura, begin."

Staring at her victim in horror, Uhura dazedly accepted the staff Lars handed her. Then full realization flooding her, she cried, "No! No! No!"

Galt's face was glacial. "It is not allowed to refuse a training exercise. Begin!"

"I don't care whether it's allowed or not! I won't do it!" And, in a fury, Uhura threw down her staff.

Very quietly, Kirk said, "None of us will do it, Galt."

Sparkle came into Galt's eyes—a glitter that reminded Kirk of the shine of snow under sun. "It is part of your training. The Providers wish it."

"The devil with the Providers!" Kirk shouted, hearing Chekov beside him mutter, "Cossacks!"

There was a pregnant pause before Galt closed his eyes—and the gems on their slave collars began to glow. The agony forced them to their knees. Then the glow faded as Galt opened his eyes. And once more there was the struggle to recover their feet.

"We have been tolerant because you are newcomers," Galt said. "But I see you must be taught a lesson." He clapped his hands sharply, and two other Thralls quickly strode from the sidelines, released their manacled fellow, all three moving away as Galt called, "Kloog!"

The hunched ape-man appeared, armed with a wide, hooked net, a dagger and a short whip. Crossing to the triangle, he faced Galt, waiting expectantly.

The *Enterprise* officers exchanged appalled glances, but the oblivious Galt merely said, "Kloog will administer correction. Uhura, take your place on that rectangle. Lars, tie her!"

She gave Kirk a frightened look and was starting forward when he swiftly interposed himself in front of her.

"*I* am responsible for the actions of my people! I demand to see the Providers!"

"That is not permitted."

Controlling the hot rage surging in him, Kirk said, "I know your Providers possess great power, but I assure you that it doesn't match the power of the entire Federation. There is a Starship searching for us now. If we're killed, you will invite the vengeance, not of one Starship, but a fleet of them."

"The Providers know of your Starfleet, Captain. And since you assume responsibility for your people, you will take the punishment." Galt smiled slightly. "If I may say so, you are rash, Captain. However, this punishment will be less painful than the collar. Turn around."

For a moment, Kirk hesitated. Then he obeyed, and Galt, still smiling, snapped manacles on him.

"You, Captain, will be target Thrall."

Well, he'd asked for it, so now he had it. Moving slowly but alertly onto the board, he paused a few feet from Kloog, half-crouched, watching the creature warily.

Galt spoke. "It's a shame to lose you, Captain. But it's worth it as an example to the others."

It was an example of insane brutality. Kloog, expert with the hooked net, lunged suddenly at the hand-bound Kirk who dodged the mesh just in time to avoid snare in it; but before he could recover himself, Kloog slashed him across the chest with his whip. Kirk, staggering backward, didn't hear Uhura's gasp of horror nor did he see Lars push back the onrushing Chekov with his spear. Fighting, he knew, for his life, he was totally concentrated on eluding the perilous net.

It lifted for another downsweep, and again Kirk ducked from under it, one of its hooks ripping his arm. Once more, whirling and crouching, the pattern of the unequal contest continued, Kirk circling, dodging as Kloog, bearing in on him, gave him not a moment's respite. He was sweating now, his legs shaking with exhaustion when Galt called, "Hold!"

Head sagging, Kirk heard him add, "Rest interval. Fifteen trisecs."

Kloog lowered his weapons, dropping down crosslegged on the floor while Kirk, staggering to a nearby bench, collapsed on it. Vaguely, he was aware that Shahna had appeared beside him and had placed a slim-necked flagon to his lips.

"This will strengthen you. Drink it."

He swallowed ravenously, some of the liquid spilling down his cut chest. Gradually, as his breathing became normal, he said, "Thanks. He's pretty fast with that whip."

"It is the net you must watch. Once you are caught in it, he will use the dagger—to finish."

He nodded; and Shahna, giving a swift glance in Galt's direction, quickly whispered, "Kloog's left eye is weak. Approach him from that side."

Startled by this unexpected concern, Kirk watched her run back to her place on the sidelines; but there was no time for reflection on its meaning, for Galt had called, "Resume places!"

However, the watchful dodging and ducking had become more confident now. As Kloog, his net and whip retrieved, turned slowly to face him, Kirk darted abruptly to the right, reversed and angled in on his opponent's left. Kloog lashed out with the whip, connecting viciously with Kirk's cheek; but he, catching the thong with a foot, jerked it from him. The net rose high for the throw. Ready for it, Kirk flung himself to the floor and, rolling, sprang up to butt Kloog in the midriff with his head. Then, swiftly, he twisted away from the net, and kicking at Kloog with both feet, felled him.

A new voice, loud and shrill, cried, "Hold!"

All the Triskelions, Galt and the Thralls, knelt, their heads bowed humbly in the direction of a blank rear wall.

"We hold, Provider One," Galt said obsequiously.

Kirk joined Chekov and Uhura, the three trying to locate the owner of the voice when it spoke again. "Provider One bids three hundred quatloos for the newcomers."

A deeper voice cried, "Provider Two bids three hundred and fifty quatloos!"

Then another one chimed in, all the disembodied voices sounding from the various walls. "Provider Three, four hundred!"

Once more the *Enterprise* officers glanced vainly around to detect some other source for the mysterious voices, the walls alone confronting them.

"Provider Two bids one thousand quatloos!"

"Provider Three says one thousand and fifty quatloos!"

It was the turn of Provider One again. "Two thousand!"

Immediately the bidding quieted. And Galt, bowing deferentially, said, "Two thousand quatloos are bid. Is there another challenge?"

The walls remained silent; and after a pause, Galt made his announcement. "The newcomers have been vended to Provider One."

Kirk spoke sharply. "We are free people. We belong to no one!"

Provider Two was pleased to approve the statement. "Such spirit! I wager fifteen quatloos that he is untrainable!"

If Kirk was spirited, so was the competitiveness of the invisible Providers. "Twenty quatloos that all three are untrainable!"

"Wagers accepted," shrilled Provider One.

Whereupon bedlam burst out from the walls, the voices overwhelming each other in their excitement to register bets on their new Thralls' trainability. The sums of offered quatloos mounted wildly until the clamor was finally stilled by the shout, "Provider Three wagers five thousand quatloos that the newcomers will have to be destroyed!"

The high, effeminate voice of Provider One shrieked, "Accepted! Mark them, Galt!"

The gems on their collars went orange.

"You now bear the mark of a fine herd," Galt said. "But I must warn you. Now that you are full-fledged Thralls, any further disobedience will be punishable by death."

The bridge's unpromising viewing screen had raised Scott's anxiety to such a pitch that he couldn't contain it. Marching purposely over to Spock, he said, "Mr. Spock, listen to me! It just doesn't make sense they could have come this far! If there's any chance at all, it's to continue to search the area where they were lost!"

Self-possessed, inscrutable, Spock said, "We searched that area, Mr. Scott."

"It's always possible to miss something!"

"Such as a failure in the Transporter mechanism?"

"No, sir. There's no sign of any failure."

"And there was no sign of them in the area of Gamma II."

McCoy broke in. "And if they weren't there, it's just ridiculous to believe they could still be alive—not after all this time!"

"In that case, Doctor, we have nothing to lose in pursuing our present course."

Quarterstaff practice had begun on the gaming board, Lars attacking, Uhura defending. As they moved away to a rhomboid, Chekov, holding a spear, was clumsily warding off Tamoon's attack.

"You must be fast, Chee-koof. Again, parry, parry. Thrust."

Anger flared in him. He swung the staff around, aiming its bladed end at a metal disk on her shoulder. It punctured the thing, and Tamoon drew back, delighted.

"That is good," she told him. "Soon you will be ready for the games. Why does that not please you, Chee-koof?"

"Chekov. The only thing that would please me is to return to the ship. How did they get us here? Where is their power, Tamoon?"

"It is not permitted to discuss." She hesitated. "Tell me of this ship. What is there so pleasing? Your Provider? Does he care for you better?"

"I have no Provider. Earth people take care of themselves."

She stared at him. "Care for themselves? But that is

55

not safe! Many things can happen! You must never return there, Chee-koof. It is not safe at all!"

Meanwhile, Shahna, laboring under the belief that Kirk's legs required exercise, had been leading him at a brisk trot through a field; and they were still trotting as they emerged from a clump of trees, side by side.

Slightly breathless, Kirk said, "We've covered over two miles. Isn't that enough? How about a breather?" And at her blank look, interpreted. "A rest."

"Oh . . . very well—if you are tired."

Kirk dropped down on the stone pediment of a ruined building; and after a pause, Shahna joined him.

Inhaling deeply, he said, "It was good to get away from that training area—even for a little while. Why do they like it, the Providers? Why do they want to watch others hurt, killed?"

The dark lashes lowered over the sapphire eyes. "It is the way."

"The voices sounded mechanical. Are they computers?"

The lashes lifted. "Computers?"

He answered his own question with another one, saying to himself, "But why, why would computers keep slaves? Shahna, have you ever seen them? Do they have bodies?"

"Not such as ours."

He looked off at the rubble of ruins at the edge of the trees. "What is that place, Shahna?"

"It is not used."

"Doesn't it have a name? It's very old. Probably built by humanoid people. Shahna, could this once have been a city of the Providers?"

Her voice shook. "I do not think it is well to ask such things."

"They have bodies," he said, "like ours . . . or they had."

She spoke firmly, almost angrily. "One does not talk of such things!"

"I see." And regretting the discomfort he'd caused

her, changed the subject. "Pretty country. Looks very much like Earth."

As all he got was another blank look, he explained. "My home planet—where I was born."

"Planet?"

Well, he thought, I can instruct too. "Have you never looked at the night sky, Shahna? The lights up there?"

"Oh, those," she said. "I *have* looked at them."

"They're stars. And around them are planets—places . . . many of them like this—with people just like us living on them."

She was staring again. "How can one live on a flicker of light?"

He smiled at her. "From Earth, Triskelion's two suns seem only a flicker of light." Then sobering, he said, "Actually, this is the darkest planet I've ever seen."

"Dark? Why, all is lighted! Here . . . the chambers . . ."

"Dark," he insisted. "Thralls have no freedom, Shahna. You can't think or do anything but what your Providers tell you."

"What else would one do?"

She *was* beautiful, and her ignorance added a quality of pathos to the beauty.

"Love, for one thing," he said.

"What is love?"

He was tempted to kiss her, but refraining, said, "On Earth, it's more important than anything else, especially between a man and a woman."

Comprehension flooded her face. "Oh, we, too, have mates. When it is time to increase the herd, my Provider will select one for me."

"On Earth, we select our own mates. Somebody we care for, love. Men and women spend their lives together—sharing things . . . making each other happy."

Flushing, she whispered, "I do not think your words are allowed."

"All right. But tell me about the Providers. Where do they live? What do they look like?"

"I have never seen them, but they are said not to be like us. They stay in—"

Suddenly, the light on her collar went into glow. Shahna gasped. Kirk leaped to his feet, and looking up at him, she just managed to whisper, "I—I have ... spoken ... of the ... forbidden. I must ... be—"

She was choking with her agony. Going to her, Kirk stood beside her in his own agony of indecision, unable to help but only to watch her slip off the pediment and sink to the ground, writhing, strangling.

He glared around him. "Stop! *I* did it! *I* made her talk!" Then his voice rose to a scream. "Stop it, I tell you! You're killing her!"

But the jewel on the collar only glowed brighter. Shahna's face darkened with the uprush of blood, her mouth opening, her clawing hands falling away from the collar. Kirk whirled to the cliff above the gaming area, shaking his clenched fist at it. *"Stop it!"* he shouted again. "She did nothing wrong! It was my fault. If you want to punish someone, punish me! Please, please . . ."

He was half-aware of a strange rustling sound like electronic laughter. Then the light on Shahna's collar winked out. As he fell on his knees beside her, a voice spoke, the high, semi-soprano voice of Provider One.

"Is that what you humans call compassion? It is interesting, but it has no value here. You present many interesting aspects, Captain. But you must learn obedience. Then you will be an excellent Thrall."

Shahna had relaxed, her lungs sucking in great gulps of air. Released from her near-fatal agony, she began to sob. Kirk took her gently into his arms.

"I know," he said. "It's all right. You're safe now here in my arms—perfectly safe. Stop crying."

She leaned her head on his shoulder, the sobs quieting. Then looking up at him wonderingly, she said, "You risked bringing their anger on yourself. Why—why did you do it?"

He held her closer. "It's the custom for Earth people to help each other when they're in trouble."

He'd known it was coming, and it came—the moment of magic between them when the mysterious shuttle moves between a man and a woman, weaving, interweaving them together in the nameless bond.

He turned her face to his and kissed her.

She drew back, startled. Then while the sapphire eyes searched his, she lifted a finger and touched his lips with it softly. "And that—was that also helping?"

Smiling, he kissed the finger. "I suppose you could call it that."

Her eyes were shining. "Please . . . help me once again."

This time the kiss grew deep, complete, and her arms lifted to go slowly around his neck. As he brushed his cheek against one, she withdrew them.

"I—I did not know it could be like this between people. Is it always so in the place you come from?"

He said, "It always should be like this for you, Shahna."

The rustle of high laughter echoed again, and Galt was abruptly with them. Silently, Kirk released the girl.

"Captain, you do indeed present many surprises. Because you have amused the Providers, there will be no punishment. Return to your quarters."

Kirk spoke softly to Shahna. "Come, we'll go together."

In the bridge command chair, Spock turned his head to the corner where Scott and McCoy were whispering together.

"Mr. Scott."

Scott started guiltily. "Yes, sir."

"Are you unable to manage anything faster than Warp Six?"

Scott moved to the command chair. "It's my opinion, sir, that we've come much too far as it is."

McCoy joined them to add his support to Scott's

opinion. "He's right, Spock. We lost Jim and the others back at Gamma II. You've dragged us a dozen light years out here on some wild hunch that—"

"I do not entertain hunches, Doctor. No transporter malfunction was responsible for the disappearance. They were not within the Gamma System. A focused beam of extremely high intensity energy was directed into the Gamma System from the binary system we are now approaching. No known natural phenomena would account for that beam. Does that not clarify the situation?"

"No, Spock, it doesn't. That's just a fancy way of saying you're playing a hunch. *My* hunch is that they're still back on Gamma II—dead or alive. And I want to make another search."

"Dr. McCoy speaks for me too, sir," Scott said.

"Gentlemen, I am in command of this vessel. We will proceed on our present course—unless it is your intention to declare a mutiny."

Spock received their glares unmoved. And for a moment, his two leading officers felt what they had often felt before: an awe of Spock. Unnumbered had been the times he had demonstrated his devotion to his Captain—a devotion now under cruel and lonely test. He would follow his own decision, unsupported, giving no sign whatever of any inward doubt of anxiety.

Scott could feel his respect for Kirk's best friend growing, suddenly. As to McCoy, he fell back on bluster.

"Who said anything about mutiny? You stubborn, pointed-eared . . . All right, but if we don't find them here, will you go back for another search of Gamma II?"

"Agreed, Doctor. Mr. Scott, now can you give me Warp Seven?"

"Aye. And perhaps a bit more."

Spock spoke to the navigator. "Warp Seven, Ensign."

Nourishment Interval. Shahna, unlocking the door of Kirk's stall, entered it without looking at him. As she set down the food container, Kirk said, "You're late."

She nodded unhappily, still evading his eyes. He rose from his bench to take the container from her. "Are you disturbed about what happened today?"

"Yes."

"Because of me?"

"You—you have made me feel very strange. If it were allowed, I would ask that you be given another Drill Thrall."

He placed the container on the cubed stand. "I wouldn't like that, darling. I wouldn't like it at all."

He opened his arms to her and she walked straight into them. For a moment, she tried to resist his lips but then hungrily responded to them. Gathering her to him more closely, he suddenly dealt her a short, hard uppercut on the chin. As she went limp, sagging in his arms, he swiftly lifted her and placed her on the bench. The key to his stall door was in her harness. He took it. Then glancing down at her, regret in his eyes, he gently kissed her forehead.

"Sorry, Shahna. Sorry, darling."

Turning quickly to the door, he pressed the key to its lock. Ten seconds later, he was at Chekov's cell, releasing him. To his whispered question, Kirk shook his head. "No, she's out cold. What about Lars and Tamoon?"

"Uhura?"

She was beside him too, now in the corridor. "I told him I didn't like the food. He's gone to report me."

Chekov said, "Tamoon won't give us any trouble, either. But I think I've killed our romance."

In Chekov's stall, the fanged creature was seated on the floor, bound with part of her own harness. A metal pot covered her head to the mouth to stifle any muffled objections.

Kirk and Chekov exchanged grins, but Uhura ran forward to make sure the corridor was deserted. It was; and the three went quickly through its archway toward the gaming area.

With lowered voice, Kirk said, "I think Galt's the only one who can operate the collars. If we can find our phasers, we can use the circuits to short the collars out."

They had passed the central triangle when the Master Thrall made one of his sudden appearances.

"Stay where you are, Captain."

As Kirk hesitated, Galt closed his eyes. For a moment, the three slave collars glowed then went out.

From a wall, their owner spoke in his unmistakable high-pitched voice. "Only a reminder, Captain. You Earthmen are most unusual . . . most stimulating."

The next moment, they were surrounded by armed, sullen-faced Thralls.

Ensign Haines was the only member of the bridge personnel who had her eyes on her console.

"Standard orbit, Mr. Spock."

Spock's eyes, like those of Scott and McCoy beside the command chair, were on the viewing screen. All watched the slowly rotating planet imaged on it.

"Sensors indicate only one concentration of life forms—in the lower hemisphere on the largest land mass." Spock's voice was toneless. "Humanoid readings, however."

"At least that gives our landing force a starting point," McCoy said.

"There will be no landing force, Doctor. Assuming that the Captain and the others are still alive, it would be unwise to endanger them by beaming down a large contingent."

"Well, we're not just going to leave them there while we sit here and wait, are we?"

Spock, leaving the command chair, was back at his scanner. Straightening, he said, "Interesting. The sensors record no power source. It might be shielded."

The strain was too much for McCoy. "Or it might

be a wild-goose chase just as we've been telling you!"

"I shall beam down," Spock said. "If I am unable to communicate, a landing force may be necessary. You must make that decision, Mr. Scott."

"Well, Spock, if you're going into a lions' den, you'll need a Medical Officer."

Getting to his feet, Spock said, "Daniel, as I recall, had only faith. But I welcome your company, Doctor. Mr. Scott, you are in command."

"Aye, sir."

Without warning, the piercing metallic voice reverberated throughout the ship. "No, Mr. Spock," said Provider One. "You will not leave the ship."

A silence, heavy as lead, fell over the bridge.

"What the de'il—" Scott began and broke off.

Miles, miles, miles below the *Enterprise*, the voice had been heard by Kirk, Chekov and Uhura on the gaming board, guarded by Lars, Tamoon, Shahna and Galt.

Provider One spoke again. "None of your control systems will operate."

Kirk was moistening his dry lips with his tongue when McCoy's familiar voice came. "Spock, what the hell is going on?"

Explanation there was none. How in the name of all the gods had the Providers arranged this simultaneous communication between their prisoners and his ship? Would his people hear him as clearly as he had heard McCoy?

Maybe. "Welcome to Triskelion, gentlemen," he said.

They *did* hear him. "Jim," McCoy cried, "is that you?"

"Yes. By now it must be obvious to you that you were expected."

Scott had been making a frantic check of controls. Finishing, he called, "It's true—what that thing said, Mr. Spock. Nothing will respond."

Now there was a slight hint of amusement in Pro-

vider One's high voice. "Commendations, gentlemen.
Your ingenuity in discovering the whereabouts of your
companions is noteworthy."

They'll be trying to locate the voice, Kirk thought—
and will fail just as we have. Well, he'd tell them what
he could.

"What you are hearing, Mr. Spock, is a Provider."

Provider One expanded his information. "We are
known to our Thralls as Providers because we provide
for all their needs. The term is easier for their limited
mental abilities to comprehend, Mr. Spock."

" 'Providing for their needs' means using Thralls—
people stolen from every part of the galaxy—to fight
each other while their owners gamble on the winner."

Spock, always charmed by the idiosyncrasies of
alien civilizations, said, "Indeed? Fascinating, Captain."

"Not in fact, Spock. These Providers lack even the
courage to show themselves."

Provider One was roused to say, "Your species has
much curiosity. However, we knew that. You are interesting in many ways."

The conversation had now become a dialogue between Kirk and his owner.

"But you *are* afraid!"

"You present no danger, Captain, while you wear
the collar. And you will wear it for the rest of your
life."

Did they hear it on the *Enterprise?*

"Then show yourselves!" Kirk shouted.

His challenge was followed by a high, electronic
whispering, followed in its turn by an acceptance of
the dare.

"There is no objection," said Provider One, and the
next instant Kirk had vanished from the gaming board.

He found himself in a circular chamber. To his left
was a crookedly shaped window, but the chief feature
of the room was a column, widened at its top to support a transparent case. Within it was what seemed to

be three blobs of protoplasm, veined and pulsating. No. Unskulled brains. Disembodied intellects, carefully preserving themselves in the satanic pride of unfeeling intellect, active only in the cause of its absolute certitudes.

Kirk left the column for the window and looked out on a vast underground complex, and too convoluted to divulge its details.

"So that's your power source," he said. "Shielded by solid rock."

"We are one thousand of your meters beneath the surface," boasted Provider One.

Back at the brain case, Kirk said, "Primary mental development . . . primitive evolution."

And was promptly corrected by Provider Two. "That is not true, Captain. Once we had humanoid forms, but we evolved beyond them."

Provider Three became self-defensive. "Through eons of devoting ourselves to intellectual pursuits, we became physically simple, the mentally superior brains you see before you."

Kirk allowed his scorn to sharpen his voice. "A species which enslaves others is hardly superior—mentally or otherwise."

He seemed to have touched Provider One on a raw place. "The Thralls are necessary to our games, Captain. We have found athletic competitions our sole diversion—the only thing which furnishes us with purpose."

"An unproductive purpose," Kirk observed. "Most unworthy of the greatest intellects in the galaxy."

The irony got through.

"We only use inferior beings."

"Inferior. Encased as you are, you don't get around much. We do. And we have found all life forms capable of superior development under proper guidance. Perhaps you're not so grandly evolved as you think."

He disconcerted them into a moment of silence

finally broken by Provider Three. "An interesting speculation, Captain. You and your people are most challenging."

"Yes, most challenging," agreed Provider Two. "It was hoped that such new blood would stimulate our stock of Thralls. How unfortunate that you must be destroyed!"

"Our destruction will only result in your own. You may control the *Enterprise,* but you cannot match the power of the entire Federation."

Another raw place in Provider One. "Your ship will be shattered to bits by a magnetic storm. No communication with your base will be possible. Your fate will remain an eternal mystery to your Federation."

Kirk gave no sign of his shocked dismay. Yet, in spite of it, he was thinking harder than he'd ever thought in his life. He laughed. "And you call yourselves 'superior'! Why, you're just run-of-the-mill murderers—killers without the spirit to *really* wager for the lives you take!"

An electronic murmur of excitement came from the case.

"Wager?" queried Provider One. "Explain yourself, Captain."

Kirk drew himself up to his full height. "My people are the most enterprising, successful gamblers in the universe. We compete for everything—power . . . fame . . . women . . . whatever we desire. It is our nature to win! I offer as proof our exploration of this galaxy."

"We are aware of your competitive abilities," pronounced Provider Three.

"Very well. Then I am willing to wager right now —and with any weapon you choose—that my people can overcome any fair number of Thralls set against them."

He'd been right. He'd caught them. Out of the case came the babble of bidding: "A hundred quatloos on the newcomers . . . two hundred against . . . four hundred against . . . five hundred for the newcomers . . . contest by multiple elimination!"

"Wait! Wait! Hear me out!" Kirk cried.

The voices stilled.

"We do not wager for trifles like quatloos! The stakes must be high!"

The silence prolonged itself until Provider One spoke. "Name your stakes, Captain."

"If my people win, the *Enterprise* and all its crew will leave here in safety. Furthermore, all Thralls on this planet will be freed."

"Anarchy! They would starve!"

Kirk ignored the comment. "They will be educated and trained by you to establish a normal, self-governing culture."

Incredulous, Provider Three cried, "Thralls—govern themselves? Ridiculous!"

"We have done this same thing with many, many cultures throughout the galaxy. Do you then confess you cannot do what we can?"

"There is nothing we cannot do," Provider Two declared.

"And if you lose, Captain?"

It was Provider One's question, but he knew that the other two were waiting intently for his answer.

There was only one to make, and he made it. "If we lose, we will stay here—the entire *Enterprise* crew—the most stubborn and determined competitors anywhere. We will become Thralls, taking part in your games and obeying all orders without rebellion. You will be assured of generations of the most exciting wagering you've ever had."

A long silence passed before Provider One said, "Your stakes are indeed high, Captain."

"Not for *true* gamesters!"

The intellects once more conferred in their electronic mumble, their decision voiced by Provider Three. "We will accept your stakes on one condition, Captain."

"Name it."

"As leader of your people, your spirit seems most indomitable. We suggest you alone—pitted against three contestants of our choosing."

"One against three? Those are pretty high odds, aren't they?"

A vein throbbed in the brain of Provider Three as it gave a small, taunting chuckle. "Not for *true* gamesters, Captain!"

Kirk shook his head. "Your terms are unfair."

"On the contrary," Provider One said. "They are extremely fair inasmuch as your alternative is death."

Kirk gave himself time—time to think, time to consider the future of the *Enterprise* crew under the domination of these intellects, time to weigh it against his own death. It had been his life, the *Enterprise* and its people. Without them, death would be welcome.

"The wager is accepted," he said.

"Galt will prepare you."

It was extraordinary, the triumph the mere brain of Provider One could infuse into its thin, shrill voice. Then as abruptly as he'd appeared in the chamber, he was back in the gaming area, standing in the center triangle, faced by Lars, Kloog, Tamoon and Shahna.

He took the staff Galt handed him. As he hefted it, gauging its weight, the sharpness of its blade, the curve of its hook, Provider One spoke from a wall.

"Because you wager your skill for all your people, they will be permitted to watch the game's outcome on the ship's viewing screen."

And at the same moment, he heard Scott shout, "Mr. Spock, look!"

All right. They knew what he felt about them. So the fact that he was willing to die to preserve them would come as no surprise. Yet he wasn't prepared for the stricken voice of McCoy. "What in the name of Heaven is—"

Scott's Highland realism spoke for him. "Heaven's got very little to do with this, Doctor."

Spock held up a hand for silence. And all of them heard Provider One.

"Captain, you will defend."

"Jim, Jim," McCoy whispered.

But Provider One had more to say.

"Thralls must stay in the blue shapes. You will take the yellow ones, Captain. Touching an opponent's color deprives a contestant of one weapon. An opponent must be killed to be removed from the game. If only wounded, he is replaced by a fresh Thrall. Is that clear, Captain?"

"Clear."

"Very well. Begin."

Galt had pushed a dagger into Kirk's belt. Then a hooked net was hung over his right shoulder and a whip shoved into his hand. Four weapons, counting the quarterstaff. But his opponents only carried one, plus their daggers. Kloog, Lars and a strange Thrall positioned themselves in the blue shapes. A very strange Thrall, a bald thing, purple-skinned, its nose two holes covered by flaps of tissue, flapping up and down over its elementary nostrils with its breathing.

Kirk started with the staff.

All three closed in on him simultaneously, forcing the *Enterprise* Captain to make a sweeping move from his yellow triangle in order to parry the bald thing's assault with its spear. Leaping from the triangle into a yellow circle, he drove Kloog into a blue hexagon. Like his physical agility, his mental ability was working faster than his opponents'.

But at once Lars had rushed him with his net, and the bald Thrall, who'd fled around a yellow square, was slashing at him with its spear blade. Cool, now that the issue was finally joined, Kirk extended the hook of his own around Lars's ankle, downing him directly into the path of the oncoming Kloog. He felled the blond giant only to see the hairless alien strike at him again with its staff blade.

A high jump lifted him from the circle, replacing him on the yellow triangle.

Back on his feet, Lars raised his net. Its meshes engulfed Kirk, catching him; and Kloog, his gorilla jaw jutted, backed off for an effective blow with his whip. Kirk, drawing his dagger swiftly, cut himself free of the tangle, and Lars, unbelievingly, stumbled, staring idiotically at his torn weapon.

Despite the bald Thrall's skill, its nose shields were flapping breathlessly. It ran up behind Kirk, snuffling like a pig at its trough; but whirling, Kirk had glimpsed a yellow pentagon to his left. He made its center and, turning, attacked the noseless thing with his staff, but it parried the strike with its own.

Kirk, however, had parried higher. Kloog, combined fear and rage inciting him, saw his chance and lashed Kirk around the body with his stinging, curling whip. Kirk's staff broke—broke in half. He wheeled, spun out of the whip, and, leaping from the pentagon, flung his staff's new-made spear at Kloog. It struck in the matted hair of his chest, drawing blood. He retreated.

Lars, with his ripped net, at once took up Kloog's position. Its uncut meshes fell over Kirk and Lars raised his dagger for the kill. Looking at the heavy blond face, merciless, Kirk said to himself, "So this is it. Okay, I die. But so does everybody else in the end."

Was it that acceptance of mortality which gave him the momentary detachment he so needed? In it, as though from a great distance, he saw the bald thing lift its spear, hurl it at him, and he ducked it. It entered Lars's stomach.

Who's to know?

There are divinites that shape our ends of which we know nothing. Vigor renewed itself in Kirk. He struggled out of the net, and the bald alien, snatching it up, yanked its dagger from its belt. Now it was armed with net, dagger and quarterstaff.

It feinted with the staff, grabbing his whip from him, but Kirk reached for it, recovered it and threw it clear of the game floor. Now it was repellently close body contact with the freak, its nose shields fluttering in Kirk's face. He wrested himself free, making another forward leap to the yellow circle.

But once more the net descended. The bald one dived at him. Somehow, he released his dagger hand, and pushing the thing aside, lashed out with his own dagger across the purple body. It collapsed, not dead, but so wounded that it couldn't rise. And at once, as Lars had been, was dragged from the field of battle by expressionless fellow Thralls, moving in from the sidelines.

Behind it, it left a thick pool of purple blood. Kirk closed his eyes against the sight. What a planet! If this insane mayhem was the result of supreme intellect, the humanoids of the galaxy would be well advised to go back to primeval seas as protozoa.

He opened his eyes. Vaulting over a blue circle, he landed on the yellow triangle's sanctuary for what he had seen was Shahna, her spear lifted, racing at him from the sidelines to challenge him.

He moved unsteadily to meet her, the muscles of his legs unreliable and barely able to clutch the splintered half of his quarterstaff.

"You lied," she said. "Everything you said . . ." and lunged at him. He fell to one knee. Then hacking his way upright, he called on all his brute strength to get under her guard and drive his blade's point into her breast.

Kill a woman in cold blood. He'd never done it. He paused, but Shahna was preparing for the death thrust, pulling back to gain impetus for another lunge at him. Then she knocked his blade aside to press her own against his heart.

Their blades crossed, bringing them face to face.

Suddenly, her lower lip began to tremble. "You— you *did* lie."

Her whispered breath was fragrant as roses. And once more the indefinable shuttle between man and woman was moving, interlacing, as mysteriously powerful as the divinities shaping our ends. Would it continue its weaving? All she'd ever known was fighting; but love? Only what he'd been able to teach her.

The dark-lashed eyes were deep in his, asking, searching.

Tears flooded the eyes. Dropping her blade, she turned to a wall, crying, "The Thralls surrender!"

He'd have to leave her, but he'd made a woman out of her. And who was to profit by her loveliness? Kloog . . . the bald horror? There were disadvantages to command of a Starship, roaming, roaming endlessly through the galaxy.

He was about to take her in his arms when he heard the voice of Provider One.

"You have won, Captain Kirk. Unfortunately. However, the terms of the wager will be honored. You are free. Remove your collars. Thralls, hear me!"

Kirk placed his hand on Shahna's collar. It came away easily. Then as he removed his own, he heard clash after metallic clash of other collars striking the floor. Shahna stared at the broken symbol of her slavery in his hand, unbelieving. Then the sapphire eyes veered to him. At the look in them, it was just as well that Galt reached them, carrying his former prisoners' phasers and communicators.

Kirk addressed a wall. "The Thralls will be trained?"

"They will be trained. We have said it, Captain Kirk."

"You may find that a more exciting game than the one you have been playing. A body is no good without a brain. But you've found a brain isn't worth much without a body."

Shahna said, "Darling."

He looked down at her. No, they could share no future. If only . . . He pulled himself together. "I didn't lie, Shahna. I only did what was necessary. Someday, you'll understand."

"I—I understand a . . . little. You will leave us now?"

He nodded, unable to speak.

"To go back to the lights in the sky? I . . . want to go to . . . those lights . . . with you. Take me."

"I can't."

"Then teach me how, and I'll follow you."

Providers, witnesses notwithstanding, he took her in his arms. "There are many things you have to learn first—things the Providers will teach you. Learn them. All your people must learn them before you can reach for the stars."

Holding her closer, he kissed her.

"Goodbye, darling, my darling."

Then he released her; and striding quickly across the board, joined the awed Chekov and Uhura. Nor did he look back as he opened his communicator.

"Beam us up, Mr. Scott."

The well-known voice said, "Aye, sir."

Alone on the board, Shahna watched the shimmer as his body went into sparkle—and he was gone with his people.

She bowed her head to hide the tears. "Goodbye, my Kirk. I will learn. And watch the lights in . . . the sky . . . and always, always remember."

So would he. But gradually—and mercifully—the memory of Triskelion's beautiful woman would begin to fade, along with the sweetness of her breath on his face.

AND THE CHILDREN SHALL LEAD
(Edward J. Lakso)

From standard orbit, the planet Triacus appeared perfectly normal, even placid. But Starfleet Command had received a distress call. No details had been included.

"Isn't Triacus where Professor Starnes and his expedition are working?" asked Captain Kirk.

Mr. Spock nodded. "It's the only M-type planet in the system. According to the records, Dr. Starnes and his colleagues found it sufficiently pleasant to bring their families along."

"Starnes taught at the Academy. I remember him— nice old fellow. And knew his stuff."

"He is a very capable scientist, Captain."

"Prepare the Transporter Room. You and I and Dr. McCoy will beam down in ten minutes."

"Certainly, Captain."

It was a dry, dusty sort of place to have chosen to set up camp. Rock formations emerged from the flat ground, the sun casting sharp shadows. The few listless shrubs were drab, except for the spatters of bright red blood.

Picks and water bottles lay scattered among the fallen bodies of men and women. Shocked, McCoy knelt to examine a crumpled shape that still held a weapon pointed at its own ruined head.

"Dr. Starnes!" Kirk's shout burst the stunned silence. Over the rock stumbled a wild-haired middle-aged man who fell to his knees as his shaking hands held a phaser pistol aimed straight at the Captain.

"Dr. Starnes! It's me, Kirk!" Unprepared, Kirk groped for his own weapon. But with an agonized twist, the man dropped and lay still. Kirk started toward him; McCoy was there before him.

"He's dead, Captain."

"He didn't seem to know me," said Kirk wonderingly. "He tried to kill me." He picked up the pistol, and nearly tripped over a woman whose body was contorted beneath her bluish face. He stooped and pried a plastic capsule from her hand. He sniffed at it doubtfully.

"Cyalodin!"

McCoy examined the capsule, then the woman. "Self-inflicted," he said briefly. "What's been going on here?"

Mr. Spock had been searching the body of the professor. Now he brought over the tricorder that had been over the shoulder of the dead man, and flipped the switch.

". . . me . . . must destroy ourselves. The alien . . . upon us, the enemy from within . . . the enemy . . ." came in a painful, choking voice. Spock snapped it off. Kirk stared around at the scene of desolation.

"All this—self-inflicted?"

McCoy nodded. "A mass suicide."

As Spock was removing the tapes from the professor's tricorder, there was a giggle. The rising trill of children's laughter sounded from behind the shrubs.

A girl and four boys poured over the rock and stopped at the sight of the *Enterprise* crew.

"Hi. Who are you?" said the tallest boy, with complete self-possession.

"Kirk, of the Starship *Enterprise*."

"I'm Tommy Starnes. This is Mary, and Steve, Ray and Don."

"Come on, play with us!" said Mary, dancing around Kirk's legs. Kirk and the others stared around them at the grisly battlefield and found themselves seized by their hands and pulled into a wild ring-around-the-rosy, pocketful of posy, and dragged into helpless crouching at "all fall down!" among the dead.

They buried the members of the Starnes exploration party in the shadow of the rock. The inscription:

STARNES EXPLORATION PARTY
STAR DATE 5039.5
IN MEMORIAM
O'Connell
Tsiku
Linden
Jaworski
Starnes
Wilkins

still glowed warm where it had been burned into the rock with phasers. Kirk reverently placed the United Federation of Planets green-and-red flag, with its circle of UFP symbols around a center of stars, upon the grave. The *Enterprise* men were respectful and silent; the burial detail had been profoundly shocked.

The children, standing in a stiff row, tried to look solemn, and succeeded only in looking bored. Steve nudged Mary restlessly. Mary whispered something in Don's ear. They glanced at Kirk.

Finally, Mary said in a not-quite whisper, "Let's go and *play!*" and the five disappeared in a flurry of shouting.

"What's the matter with them? No sign of grief at all," said Kirk.

"No, Jim, no indication of any kind," said McCoy gravely.

"Or fear?"

"They *seem* completely secure and unafraid. But it's possibly the effect of traumatic shock."

"I can't believe it. For a child to suppress the fact that both parents are dead . . ."

The dry voice of Spock remarked, "Humans do have an amazing capacity for choosing what they wish to believe—and excluding that which is painful."

"Not children, Spock. Not to this extent. It's incredible."

"What those children saw is incredible, Jim." McCoy was quietly insistent. "The way these deaths occurred, any reaction is possible, including lacunar amnesia. That's my diagnosis, until specific tests can be made."

Kirk shook his head. "I'll have to be guided by that for the present, Doctor. But surely I can question them."

"No. Certainly not until the fabric of traumatization has weakened, or you can find another explanation for their behavior. Forcing them to see this experience now could cause permanent damage. Such amnesia is a protection against the intolerable."

Kirk had to accept this. "But, Bones, whatever happened here is locked up inside those children."

The cheerful sounds of children at play had been present throughout. Now Tommy was tying a blindfold around the eyes of Steve, the smallest boy, and the others dashed for cover behind the rocks as Tommy turned him round and round. As Steve began to grope, Tommy tiptoed backward softly—and tripped. Steve jumped gleefully on top, crying, "Tommy, Tommy! I caught you!" The others danced out of hiding, shouting all at once.

Kirk detached Steve from Tommy's back and helped the tall boy to his feet.

"Hurt yourself?"

"Nah. I'm okay." The others were trying to reach Tommy's head with the blindfold.

"It's Tommy's turn, it's Tommy's turn!"

It was all Kirk could do to outshout them. "Children! It's time to leave here and go up to the ship."

"Oh, no, not yet. We're just beginning to have some fun! Not now, please?" came a chorus of protest.

Kirk searched their faces for some other reaction.

"I'm sorry. It's getting late. You'll have to go with Dr. McCoy."

But all they did was grumble, disappointed. "Only five more minutes, huh, please? It's still Tommy's turn and everything! . . . And I didn't have a turn yet . . ."

McCoy took charge of them. They didn't look back toward the camp at all.

Kirk and Spock stood for a moment by the graves. The flag fluttered peacefully.

"If it's not lacunar amnesia that's blanking out their minds, there may be something here that is doing it."

"The attack on Professor Starnes's party must surely have been unprovoked," said Spock musingly.

"Attack? It seems to be mass suicide."

"I stand corrected, Captain. 'Induced' would be a more precise term. Induced by an outside force."

Alert, Kirk said, "Such as?"

"The release of bacteria. Or a helpless mental depression. A state of suicidal anxiety. These could be chemically induced."

"What would make the children immune?"

"I do not know. But it is a possibility, Captain. A severe form of schizophrenia leading to a helpless depressive state could be chemically created."

"With the children intentionally free."

Spock nodded. "A valid hypothesis."

"We shall have to investigate this place more thoroughly. We'll go aboard now."

Animals and children start off on the right footing in a new environment when provided immediately with a little something to stave off the pangs of starvation. Nurse Christine Chapel mounted an expedition to the Commissary. When it comes to ice cream flavors, a computer can outdo a fairy godmother.

"All right, children," said Christine, holding out a fistful of colored cards. "Each color means a different flavor. Take your pick and the computer will mix it; just call out your favorite."

The five voices clamored in urgent delight. "Orange-vanilla-cherry-apricot-licorice-CHOC'LIT!" she handed two cards to each child. Four of them dashed to the insert slot and jammed their cards in. The smallest, Steve, was clearly stuck. His face conveyed agonies of indecision.

"Would you like to be surprised, Stevie?" asked Nurse Chapel gently.

Relieved, he nodded. She inserted two cards at random. The read-out panel twinkled and the computer hummed, and eagerly Steve opened the little window and withdrew a heaping dish.

He looked up at her from somewhere around her knees with tear-filled eyes. He said sorrowfully, "But it's coconut and vanilla. It's all *white!*"

She patted him. "There, there now, Stevie. There are unpleasant surprises as well as pleasant ones. That was your unpleasant surprise. Now what would you like for the pleasant one?"

There is nothing like knowing what you don't want, after all, for clarifying a decision. Stevie said, loud and clear, "Chocolate wobble and pistachio."

"Coming right up." The crisis was past.

"And peach."

Trying not to think about it, Christine submitted the required cards to the machine. "Oh, this is going to be a wonderful surprise."

Not vastly surprised, Steve accepted the huge mound of colors with satisfaction and trotted off to join the others at the table. The clinking of spoons and chatter overwhelmed the voices of Kirk and McCoy, who stood watching in the doorway.

"The tests show no evidence of tension due to lying," said McCoy glumly. "They behave as if nothing were wrong. Physically, they check out completely sound. And there's no sign of any biochemical substance to account for their present state. I have no answers, Jim."

"There has to be an answer." Kirk stared at the laughing group, absorbed in ice cream.

"Why can't it wait till we get to Starbase Hospital, where they can be checked by a child specialist? I'm no pediatrician."

"We're not leaving here till I know what went on—or what's going on."

McCoy shrugged. "Well, I won't *forbid* you to question them. But it could harm them."

"It could be far worse for them if I don't—and for us too."

McCoy gave him an uncertain glance. "Be careful, Jim."

Kirk nodded and eased his way over to the table, where there was much scraping of last bits from bottoms of bowls.

". . . and after this we can play games," Christine Chapel was saying cheerfully.

"Mmmm, yeah . . . that was fun . . . some *more* . . ." surfaced from the general babble.

"Well, well," said Kirk, smiling. "You seem to be having such a good time over here, I think I'll join you. Is that all right?"

"Please do," said Mary formally.

"I'll have a dish too—a little one. A very little one," he said to Christine.

"Of course."

"*Very* little," he said meaningfully. And then to the children, "This is better than Triacus, isn't it?"

Five faces turned to him with the look of disappointed resignation that children give to hopeless adults.

"That dirty old planet?" said Don scornfully.

Ray's snub nose wrinkled so hard as to nearly disappear. "What's to like about that place?"

Mary explained. "You weren't there very long, Captain. You don't know."

"I don't think your parents liked it much either."

"Yes, they did," said Tommy quickly, echoed by, "Mine sure did. Mine too."

Don summed it up. "Parents like stupid things."

Christine Chapel saw an opportunity. "I don't know about that. Parents like children."

"Ha," said Mary. "That's what you think."

"I'm sure your parents loved you," said Kirk. "That's why they took you with them all the way to Triacus, so you wouldn't be so far away for so long a time. That would have made them unhappy; they would miss you. Wouldn't you miss them too?"

The children looked at each other, and away. They squirmed. Tommy looked thoughtful for a split second and then said, grinning, "Bizzy! Bizzy, bizzy!"

It exploded into laughter as they all joined in. "Bizzy-bizzy-bizzy-bizzy . . ." They jumped up and chased around the room, bumping each other and shouting, "Bizzy, bizzy, bizzy!" Don called, "Guess what we are?"

"A swarm of bees!" said Christine.

They shook their heads and screamed with laughter. Mary's voice rose above them all, crying, "Watch out! I'll sting you!"

"A swarm of adults," said Kirk softly. The laughter missed a beat, and rose shrilly. Kirk caught Mary as she careened into him with a face of near-fury. "Now wait a minute . . ."

Tommy said hastily, "Can we have some more ice cream, please?"

"I don't think so," said Kirk, slowly releasing the little girl. "It would spoil your dinner."

"See what I told ya? They *all* say it." The children gathered behind Tommy, who stood there, a young captain ready to defend his crew, Kirk thought. The boy was a leader. But why this . . . sense of opposition?

"All right, children," he said. "You've had a full day. I think you could use some rest. Nurse Chapel will see you to your quarters."

"A very good idea, Captain," said Christine with some relief. There had been tension building up in the room. She herded them toward the door through the "Awwws" and "Do we have tos."

Kirk called to Tommy. "Just a moment. I'd like to ask you something." McCoy had quietly joined the

Captain at the table. Tommy reluctantly sat down on the other side.

"Tommy, will you tell me what you saw?"

"Saw where?"

"By the rocks. On Triacus."

Tommy shrugged. "You were there," he said indifferently.

"Did you see your father today?"

"I saw'm."

"Did he seem upset?"

"Yeah, he was very upset."

"What about?"

"I didn't ask him." How could he get through this almost sullen resistance and reach the boy?

"What was going on that would have upset him?"

Tommy looked at Kirk distantly. "How should I know? He was always upset. Just like you, Captain Kirk."

"I'm not upset with you or your friends, Tommy. We invited you aboard the *Enterprise*. Why would I do that if I didn't like you?"

"You had your reasons," said the boy in a voice too old for him.

Kirk tried another tack. "Are you unhappy about leaving Triacus?"

"That place? That's for adults."

"Aren't you sorry about . . . about leaving your parents?"

"My parents?" said Tommy, amazed. "They love it down there. Always bizzy. They're happy." He wriggled to his feet. "Can I please go now? I'm tired too, you know."

Kirk sighed. "Yes, certainly. I'll take you."

"I know the way."

They let him go. "Round one to the young contender," said McCoy.

"Almost a knockout," agreed Kirk. "It's as if the parents were strangers to them. But—" he flipped the switch on the communicator. "Kirk to Security. Post a guard on the children. They're to be kept under constant watch."

But neither officers, guards nor crew heard the soft sound of chanting from Tommy's room:

> *Hail, hail, fire and snow,*
> *Call the angel, we will go,*
> *Far away, far to see,*
> *Friendly angel, come to me.*

Perhaps they were saying their prayers.

Kirk passed a restless night. The memory of little Mary dancing on her mother's grave kept returning to haunt him. If he had not seen the tragedy, he would never have suspected any trouble at all from the children's attitude. It was all very well to talk of lacunar amnesia, but there was an undercurrent of horror that he could not shake.

And the doctor had found no signs of Spock's "chemically induced" derangement.

The viewscreen on the bridge showed the expected image of Triacus, just distant enough for the details of the landscape to be blurred.

"Mr. Sulu?"

"Maintaining standard orbit, Captain," said Sulu, pleased to give an "all's well" report to the tired face of his commander.

"Lieutenant Uhura, is there any report from the planet security team?"

"Everything is quiet, sir." Everything quiet, everything in order. Why this sense of unease?

Mr. Spock appeared at his elbow. "Captain, I have extracted the salient portion of Professor Starnes's tapes."

"Good." Kirk moved to Spock's console.

"Among the technical facts he gathered, Professor

Starnes also offers some rather . . . unscientific hypotheses." Spock's voice expressed distrust.

"Let's see them, Mr. Spock."

" . . . *Log date, 5025.3. Ever since our arrival on Triacus, I've had a growing feeling of uneasiness.* The distinguished man on the screen glanced around him. *"At first, I attributed it to the usual case of nerves commonly associated with any new project. However, I found that the rest of my associates were also bothered by these anxieties."*

Kirk and Spock exchanged a puzzled glance. On the screen, Dr. Starnes licked his lips and hurried on.

"The only ones not affected are the children, bless them, who are finding the whole thing an exciting adventure." For a moment, the trouble left his face and he smiled. *"Ah, to be young again!"*

"Are there more of these unscientific hypotheses, Mr. Spock?"

Spock nodded briefly.

" . . . *5032.4 The feeling of anxiety we've all been experiencing is growing worse. It seems to be most intense close to the camp, in fact. There is a cave in the rocks in which we have been sheltering part of the time; I have ordered Professor Wilkins to begin excavating. There are signs that the area was once inhabited, and perhaps there is an explanation to be found."*

Spock switched off the tricorder. "There is another portion, Captain, which I believe you'll find particularly interesting." He adjusted the mechanism.

" . . . *5038.3 Professor Wilkins completed his excavation today. Although whatever civilization that might have been here was destroyed by a natural catastrophe, as described in notebooks 7 through 12 of our records, it would appear that . . . took refuge in the cave . . . all our efforts, we are becoming more apprehensive . . . as if some unseen force . . . influ- . . ."* The recording had gradually begun fading and bleeping. Now the professor's mouth went on moving, but only a high whistling emerged from the tricorder. As Spock bent over it to try to adjust the settings, even the image blurred.

"What happened?" said Kirk.

"Unknown," replied Spock, frowning over his instrument. Kirk heard a soft step behind him.

Tommy smiled, all boyish freckles.

"I didn't see you come in, Tommy," said Kirk.

"I had something to say to you, Captain. After we leave here, can you take us to Marcos Twelve?"

"No, Tommy, we'll probably take you to a Federation Starbase."

Urgently, Tommy said, "But I have relatives on Marcos Twelve."

"I'm sorry, but Marcos Twelve isn't within our patrol area. Mr. Spock, we'll continue in my quarters." Spock was still inspecting the tricorder. He now removed the tape.

"Oh, Captain," said Tommy, looking wonderingly around the bridge at the consoles, the flashing lights, the complex equipment. "Can I stay here and watch?" For a moment, Kirk forgot the problem the boy represented, and remembered his own enchantment the first time he had been taken aboard a Starship. "I'll be very quiet," the boy added hopefully.

"All right, Tommy. Lieutenant Uhura, please ask Dr. McCoy to report to my quarters for a brief conference."

The last Kirk saw of Tommy, he was heading for Kirk's own chair—going to play Captain. Kirk smiled at Mary as he and Spock passed her at the door.

"I wonder where the rest of them are?"

"Playing, no doubt," said Spock, still looking at the malfunctioning tricorder as they walked. "It seems to be a thing they do. Most illogical."

"Of course, Mr. Spock."

Mr. Scott woke up ten minutes late and just a little irritated with himself. He stomped to the Engineering

Room and picked up his clipboard, glaring at the two technicians who were on duty. Suddenly, he stopped dead in front of an indicator.

"And when did we change course?"

One of the technicians turned and looked at him curiously. "We haven't changed course."

"What d'ye mean we haven't changed course? Look at your bridge control monitor!"

Mildly puzzled, the technician replied, "We're still in orbit, sir."

"Have you gone completely blind? Tha's no' orbiting position!" Scott reached over to the controls.

The technician seized his hand and thrust it aside. "Don't touch the controls, sir," he said quietly.

"What the devil d'ye think ye're doin'?" Scott snatched his hand back.

"We must remain in this orbit until the bridge orders are changed."

"You blind fuil, can't ye see what's in front of ye? We're not *in* orbit!" Mr. Scott lunged toward the controls again.

"I will not disobey an order from the bridge," reiterated the technician firmly. He placed himself squarely before the console, barring Scott.

"You *are* disobeying an order from the bridge! Now step aside!" What ailed the man? Triacus was nowhere in sight; the readings showed the *Enterprise* moving through space at Warp Two.

"You're losing control of yourself, sir," said the second technician carefully and very gently.

"Not yet!" Scott's voice had become a growl as he drew back his fist. He ducked the blow aimed at his chin and connected satisfyingly with the solar plexus of the first technician, who doubled up and backed away. The second man was on Scott at once, and furiously Scott swung and knocked him down.

Unfortunately, the first man had recovered and dispatched Mr. Scott with a neat blow from behind. The two technicians glanced at his fallen body and turned back to their consoles.

Little Don stared down at the big man lying on the floor. His white teeth flashed in a proud grin.

In Kirk's quarters, the tricorder was functioning again.

"*. . . I'm being influenced to do things that don't make sense. I've even gone so far as to call Starfleet Command to request a spaceship to be used as a transport.*" Professor Starnes had entirely lost composure; his eyes had grown dull in deep caverns under his brows. "*It was only when I couldn't tell them what I wanted to transport that I began to realize that my mind was being . . . directed. I decided to send a dispatch to Starfleet, warning them. . . . God forgive us! We must destroy ourselves . . . The alien is upon us! The enemy from within, the enemy . . .*" The cracked voice faded.

"He never completed the entry. And that dispatch was never sent—only scenes of family life, games and picnics with the children. That is the complete record." Spock was sober as he rewound the tapes. "Whatever overwhelmed them must have done so with incredible speed, or the professor would have provided details of the experience. He was an excellent scientist and tireless in the pursuit of the truth."

"A high tribute coming from you, Mr. Spock. But that could be what destroyed him."

Spock stared at Kirk. "The truth destroy? I don't follow that, Captain. It seems to be a non sequitur. The pursuit of truth is the noblest activity."

"Of course, of course. But the revelation of truth had often been fought, and fought hard."

"He's only too right, Spock," said McCoy.

"Unfortunately, I am compelled to agree. Evil seeks to maintain power by the suppression of truth." Slowly, Spock added, "Or by misleading the innocent."

With a sense of nearing enlightenment, Kirk said, "I wonder . . . ?"

"Do you mean the children?" said McCoy.

"Yes, Doctor."

There was a short silence, broken by the Captain. "Spock, what do we know about the race that lived here?"

"Legends, Captain. They say that Triacus was the seat of a band of marauders who made constant war throughout the system of Epsilon Indi. After many centuries, these destroyers were themselves destroyed by those they had preyed upon."

"Is that the end of it?"

"No. Like so many legends, this too has a frightening ending. It warns that the evil is awaiting a catalyst to set it in motion once again and send it marauding across the galaxy."

The three officers looked at one another. "Is it possible that this . . . evil . . . has found its catalyst?"

"I was speaking of a legend, Captain," said Spock severely.

"But most legends have their bases in fact, Mr. Spock."

"I think I read you, Jim," said McCoy. "But as Medical Officer, I must warn you that unless the normal grief is tapped and released from these children, you're treading dangerously."

"I'll respect your diagnosis, Bones. But not to the exclusion of the safety of the *Enterprise*. Thank you. Mr. Spock, what other expeditions have visited Triacus?"

"According to Federation records, this is the first."

"What was that about an 'unseen force'? Starnes said it was influencing him, he had recognized and was beginning to fight it . . ."

"And he had canceled his request for a ship," said Spock.

"The ship! Yes, a ship for Triacus. But why? Transport was wanted, but by whom?"

With decision, Kirk addressed the communicator. "Security Detachment. Ready for relief duty on Triacus. Assemble in the Transporter Room immediately." He added, more to himself than to the others, "I'll have some questions for the first detachment as soon as they've beamed up. It's about time we found out whether Starnes's 'enemy within' is on the planet below—or here on board."

In the Transporter Room, two guards were already standing on the platform. Spock went to the controls. As Captain Kirk told the men that their tour of duty would be one hour, they looked at each other with astonishment—and then uneasiness. "Be ready with your communicators at all times to report any signs of alien beings. Don't wait to investigate. Is that clear?" The men nodded. "Beam down the guards."

Mr. Spock pulled the lever; the guards shimmered, began to fade and were gone. "Beam up the Seucurity Detachment from Triacus."

The flickering figures on the platform faded, returned, faded. Where there should have been two solid security guards, there was only scintillating light.

"What's wrong?" said Kirk sharply.

"I am unable to lock on to the proper coordinates, Captain."

"Why not?"

"It appears we are no longer orbiting Triacus."

"But that's impossible." As the information sank in, Kirk said with horror, "If we're not orbiting Triacus, those men I just beamed down are dead."

"Captain, we are no longer orbiting Triacus."

"Activate the bridge monitor screen." Mr. Sulu was sitting placidly at his console, with Tommy watching interestedly. Uhura was smiling at little Mary. "Captain to bridge. Mr. Sulu, we are not in orbit around Triacus."

"With all respects, Captain," replied Sulu, surprised, "you're wrong. I have Triacus on my screen right now."

"You're off course. I'm coming up there."

He merely glanced at the children as he hurried to Sulu's station, followed by Spock.

"Mr. Sulu, your controls are not in orbiting position."

"But we *are* in orbit. Look." The screen showed the planet serenely below them.

"So it would appear," said Spock.

Behind them, the children had begun to play some game. Mary's voice chanted, *"Hail, hail, fire and snow . . ."* as the other three gathered in the doorway. They formed a circle and joined hands, clasping and unclasping in a complicated pattern. Kirk was aware of them only as a background distraction.

"Mr. Scott! This is Kirk. Look at your course override. What is our heading?"

The answer came blandly through the intercom. "Marcos Twelve, Captain."

Marcos Twelve! Kirk glanced at the circle of children. " . . . *Far away, far to see . . ."*

"Why have you changed course, Mr. Scott?"

"According to your order, Captain." The intercom clicked off.

" . . . Friendly angel, come to me . . ."

"Mr. Scott! Scotty!"

The lights on the bridge dimmed slightly and took on a greenish tinge. In the circle of children, something was forming in the air, not with the familiar shimmer of a transporter beam, but eerily, gradually, the figure of a silver-haired, sweet-faced manlike being clad in a glittering cloak took shape. It spoke to the children.

"You have done well, my friends. I, Gorgan, am very proud. You have done what you must do. As you believe, so shall you do."

Softly, the children replied in chorus, *"As we believe, so shall we do."*

"Marcos Twelve has millions of people on it. Nearly a million will be our friends." The figure smiled benignly. *"The rest will become our enemies. Together with our friends, we will destroy them as we destroyed our enemies on Triacus."* It glowed with satisfaction. *"A million friends from Marcos Twelve will make us invincible. We can do anything we wish in the whole*

universe. It will be all ours to play in, and no one can interfere. All ours, my friends!"

It spread out its hands. *"Now we have come to a moment of crisis. The enemy has discovered our operation. But they are too late! They no longer control the ship—we do. We shall prevail! They will take us wherever we desire.*

"As you believe, so shall you do."

The children, gazing raptly at the figure, replied, *"As we believe, so shall we do."*

"Each of you will go to your stations. Maintain your controls. If resistance comes, you know what to do. Call upon their Beasts! Their Beasts will serve us well. In each one of our enemies is the Beast which will consume him.

"Remember how it was on Triacus? If they resist, so shall it be on the Enterprise. *If you need me, call me, and I, Gorgan, will appear. We make ready for our new beginning on Marcos Twelve. We must not falter . . .*

"As you believe, so shall it be, so shall it be. . . ."
The creature smiled sweetly upon the children and slowly faded.

Mr. Spock's eyebrow lifted in astonishment. Kirk was unable to move for a paralyzed moment, and in that moment, Tommy whispered orders to the others.

"Go to your stations. Mary, you remain here with me." Don, Steve and Ray whisked out the door as Mary seated herself near Uhura.

Kirk spoke gently to Sulu. "Helmsman, disregard what you see—whatever you think you see—on your screen. Set a course for Starbase 4." Sulu's hands jerked. He froze, blood draining from his face as he stared at the screen.

"Helmsman, do you hear me?"

Sulu managed to whisper, "Yes, sir." Kirk, relieved, ignored Tommy's mutter.

". . . See, see, what shall he see . . ." The boy's eyes glittered with concentration.

"Lieutenant Uhura, contact Starbase 4. Tell them we are bringing the children back. Tell Starfleet Command that I suspect them of being alien in nature and I want a thorough investigation made on our arrival."

"Aye, aye, sir," said Uhura briskly and turned to her board. She stopped. She began shivering as her hands went to touch her face, her eyes fixed on her console.

"Lieutenant!" said Kirk sharply. Then more gently, "What are you staring at?" Uhura moaned.

"My death," whispered the beautiful Bantu. "A long, long death. Ancient with disease and pain. Disease and death." Her voice rose to a scream. "I see my death!"

Kirk stared at her console. For a fleeting second, he saw Uhura's face, hideously disfigured and nearly bald, a gray mass of wrinkles. But as he blinked, the station was its usual neat assembly of equipment.

"There's nothing there but your communicators," he said.

She was whimpering. "God help me. Please don't let it, Captain. Don't let it be!"

Kirk's glance fell on Mary, hunched up in total concentration. She was singing very softly. "*. . . shall she see . . . a dying old hag where a girl should be . . .*"

Uhura moaned, touched her smooth young face and stared in paralyzed horror.

"Spock, you make the call to Starfleet." Kirk turned helplessly away from Uhura's anguish, only to see Sulu's eyes staring wildly at his screen.

"Sulu, I ordered you to change course!" Kirk strode to the station and reached for the controls.

Sulu struck his hand away. "Captain! Sir!" His eyes never strayed from his screen. "Stay away from the controls! Or we'll be destroyed!"

"But Mr. Sulu, there's nothing there!" said Kirk angrily.

"Can't you see them? The missiles? They're coming at us by thousands!"

"There are no missiles, Mr. Sulu." Kirk reached for the console. Sulu struck him away.

"Leave them alone! If we touch anything, we will be hit! You'll kill us all!"

Spock's voice came coolly from behind him. "Captain, why are we bothering Starfleet?"

What had happened to his crew? Could nobody take an order at all—even Spock? His First Officer met his look defiantly.

"This bridge is under complete control," said Spock. "There's no need to alert Starfleet."

"Take a look around you," said Kirk. Sulu, staring fixedly at his viewscreen, blind to everything but the terror-image before him; Uhura, crouching in agony at her console; and Tommy, whose freckled boy-face had taken on a look of unrelenting hardness. Spock closed his eyes. Kirk watched him anxiously as he stood shuddering very slightly, fighting to regain control of his mind.

Tommy too began to shudder. Spock opened his eyes and returned to the Communications station. He reached for the instruments. His hands stopped.

"I cannot obey your order, Captain," he said.

Kirk opened the intercom. "Send up two security guards." When they appeared in the doorway, he said, Take Mr. Sulu to his quarters."

The guards looked at him blankly.

"You wanted us, sir?"

"Take Mr. Sulu to his quarters. Now!" The guards simply stood there, looking bewildered. Kirk began to grow angry. "I gave you an order. Take Mr. Sulu to his quarters at once and don't just stand there like a couple of . . . What the hell's the matter with you?" The guards looked at one another and shrugged.

"Must be some sort of joke," said one.

Kirk shouted furiously. "Can't you hear me? I will have my orders obeyed immediately, d'you hear?" He lunged at the guard. The man shoved him back calmly and the two coolly departed. Kirk started after them, only to find himself restrained by Mr. Spock. He stood for a moment, undecided. His eye fell on Tommy.

Kirk knew who to blame for this mess. He strode toward the boy, his hand raised. If ever any kid was asking for a good walloping . . .

And he couldn't do it. He couldn't hit a little boy. The little boy smiled with satisfaction.

Kirk turned back to Spock. His knees buckled in reaction to the waves of adrenalin that had been pouring through him. He had to hold Spock's arm for support.

"Captain, we must get off this bridge." Spock guided him, stumbling, into the elevator.

Kirk felt cold sweat on his forehead. Not even Spock obeyed orders. The ship was out of control. His crew had gone mad, or mutinous. He was losing command, even of his own legs. Fear grew in him, and he lurched, clinging to Spock. He couldn't trust Spock, though. He couldn't trust anyone. He couldn't command a single crewman. He had lost the *Enterprise*.

"I'm losing command," he muttered, sweating again, the heat of fear overcoming the coldness. His legs were strong, strong, but wouldn't hold him up. He stared at the treacherous satanic face of his First Officer. "I'm alone, I'm alone. This ship . . . it's sailing on and on . . . without me . . ." He touched the wall of the elevator, trying to get a grip on it. "I'm losing command. I'm losing command! My ship . . . my ship . . ."

"Captain."

"I've lost the *Enterprise*. No . . . no . . ." he sobbed. Spock caught him as he sagged, and held him upright.

"Jim."

The shock of that voice calling him by name was a shower of cold water. Slowly, the hysteria began to ebb.

"I've got command?" he whispered, looking to the Vulcan for reassurance. Spock nodded with vast conviction.

"I've got command." Kirk's own voice was regaining strength.

"Correct, *Captain*," said Spock firmly, allowing no further doubt. "I am awaiting orders, *Captain*. Where to?"

Kirk tested his legs. They were steady. He let go of Spock and stood up. ". . . *in each one . . . is the Beast which will consume him*." Well, he had met his Beast. So had Spock. Between them they had conquered the enemies within—themselves. Now the enemy within the *Enterprise* remained.

"To Auxiliary Control, my Vulcan friend. This ship is off course."

They entered the Engineering Room. Scotty looked up, smiled blandly and nodded.

"Mr. Scott. I want you to override the bridge navigation system and plot a course for Starbase 4."

"I can't do that, sir!" said Scott with indignation.

"Why not?"

"These are vurra sensitive instruments. I'll no' have you upsetting their delicate balance." There was a hint of panic underlying the burring voice. "There'll be no tamperin' with the navigation system of this ship, Captain."

"I'm not asking you to tamper with it. I'm ordering you to plot a course!"

"You're ordering suicide. We'd all be lost, forever lost!" Scott grabbed a wrench from the tools stacked nearby. The two technicians loomed supportively behind him.

Spock looked at the corner of the room. Steve was quietly watching.

"I've given you men an order," said Kirk.

Scott crouched over his console, brandishing the wrench.

"You go 'way now. Go away or I'll kill you!" Kirk could not believe such words coming from his Chief Engineer, who was coming more and more to resemble a caveman with upraised club.

"Scotty, listen to me," the Captain urged. "The *Enterprise* has been invaded by alien beings. Its destination is now Marcos. If we go there, millions will die, the way they died on Triacus."

Scott snarled and lunged. The technicians jumped Spock, undeterred by his strength. Neither Spock nor Kirk was prepared to inflict serious damage on the men, but the Engineering crew had no such qualms. At last, thanks to the Vulcan nerve pinch and some quick dodging, they managed to make their way to the elevator.

Spock stared searchingly at Kirk. Still panting from the scuffle, Kirk knew what the question was.

"It's all right, Spock. My . . . Beast . . . is finished. It won't return."

Spock acknowledged this with a nod. "But, Captain, as long as those children are present, there is danger. They are the carriers."

Sometimes, Kirk thought, Spock was more human than at other times.

"But they're children, Spock. Not alien beings. Only children, being misled."

"They are followers. Without followers, evil cannot spread."

This was definitely one of the other times. "They're *children*," Kirk said helplessly.

"Captain, the four hundred and thirty men and women on board the *Enterprise,* and the ship itself, are endangered by these . . . *children.*" Spock was grim.

"They don't understand the evil they're doing."

"Perhaps that is true. But the evil within them is spreading fast, and unless we can find a way to remove it—"

Reluctantly, Kirk faced it. "We'll have to kill them." He knew Spock was right. As they turned the corner, the way was blocked.

Ensign Chekov, armed with a phaser and flanked by three crewmen, stood in front of them.

"Captain Kirk," said Chekov nervously.

"What is it, Ensign?"

"I have been instructed to place you and Meester Spock under arrest."

"By whose order?"

"Starfleet Command, sir." With his free hand, he thrust a printed communication at the Captain, who glanced at it and looked back at the young officer.

"Where did you hear this order?" Chekov's face was working with some inner torment. Down the corridor, Tommy waited.

"Now listen to me," said Kirk firmly. "This order is false. I want you and your men to return to your stations."

"I am sorry, Captain, but I must inseest that you and Meester Spock come weeth me to the detention section."

"Listen to me!" said Kirk, taking a step toward him. The rifle rose and pointed at his heart.

"Do not force me to keel you, sir. I weel if I have to," said Chekov desperately. Heavy perspiration ran down his forehead. "Will you come peacefully?"

"*Listen* to me. This is a false order."

"I have never disobeyed an order, Captain," cried Chekov. "Never, never!"

"I know that, Ensign. You have never disobeyed an order. But an alien being is aboard this ship—"

"I cannot disobey, I cannot disobey an order," wailed Chekov, the rifle wavering. Spock had worked his way around the group and suddenly seized the weapon. It was a signal for the other crewmen to attack, and once again Kirk and Spock found themselves entangled in flying fists and vicious blows.

Tommy watched, concentrating and strained, as the rifle traveled from hand to hand.

Suddenly, Spock emerged from the melee holding the phaser. Tommy had vanished.

Feeling his bruises, Kirk said, "Mr. Spock, take these men to detention and then join me on the bridge." Spock gestured with the phaser and the others slowly started moving, looking dazed.

The bridge was as he had left it: Uhura rocking back and forth, keening, Sulu staring.

"Marcos Twelve in sight, sir," he said dully.

"Mr. Sulu, we are not going to Marcos Twelve. I want you to change course."

"No, Captain, no!" As Kirk approached the console, Sulu drew his pistol.

"Sulu, there is no collision possible. It's being planted in your mind, on your screen."

Sulu growled. Kirk stopped, startled. Spock and McCoy entered on this tableau.

"The prisoners are in the deten . . ." Spock's voice trailed off as he took in the impasse at Sulu's console. He stepped toward Kirk. Sulu raised his pistol to cover both of them.

"Stand back, Mr. Spock."

Kirk nodded. Then he looked at Mary, and at Tommy.

"The *Enterprise* will never reach Marcos Twelve. You will not be landed there."

"The crew will take us," said Tommy contemptuously. "The crew believe us."

"The crew! They don't understand. When they understand as I do, they will not take you to Marcos."

"They will!" cried Mary passionately. "They-will-they-will-they-will!"

Tommy's head was high. "We are going to Marcos. We are all going to Marcos. The crew will follow our friend."

Kirk spoke compassionately. "Your friend. Oh, yes, your friend. Where is that stowaway? Why does he hide?"

"He'll come if we call him," said Mary stoutly.

"But we won't," Tommy broke in. "We don't need him. We're not afraid of you."

"Good," said Kirk. "I'm glad you're not afraid of me. But your . . . er . . . leader is afraid. What's he so afraid of?"

"He's not afraid of anybody!"

"He's not afraid of anything!"

"He's afraid to be seen. When the crew see and hear him, they will know he is not their friend, and they will no longer follow."

Tommy shouted, "He *is* our friend!"

"Then let him show himself. Bring him out. Let him prove that he's MY friend and I'll—I'll follow him to Marcos Twelve and the end of the universe!"

"No!" cried Tommy. He was beginning to doubt.

An idea struck Kirk. "Mr. Spock, play back the chant. The one the children sang before, when the alien appeared." Unmistakably, Spock conveyed approval. Dr. McCoy shook his head doubtfully.

The chant began:

> *Hail, hail, fire and snow,*
> *Call the angel, we will go,*
> *Far away, far to see,*
> *Friendly angel, come to me.*
>
> *Hail, hail, fire and snow . . .*

As the chant replayed, Steve, Don and Ray came in slowly. The children drew into a group. This time, they didn't seem to want to join hands.

"The time has come to see the world as it is," said Kirk.

The shimmering form of the alien began to gather strength.

"Who has summoned me?" The deep resonant voice penetrated even the nightmare in which Uhura was lost.

"I did, Gorgan. My Beast has gone. It lost its power in the light of reality. I command again. And I ordered you here." It was high time, thought Kirk, that we met this antagonist face to face.

The alien smiled with infinite sweetness. *"No, Captain. I command here. My followers are strong and faithful. And obedient."* He beamed on the children, who huddled closer tgether. *"That is why we can take what is ours, wherever we go."*

Spock said, "You can only take from those who do not know you."

"And we know you," said Kirk.

"Then you know I must win, Captain."

"Not if we join together to fight you."

The alien shook its silver head calmly. *"Foolish, foolish. You will be destroyed. I would ask you to join me, but you are too gentle. A grave weakness."*

"We are also very strong."

"But your strength is neutralized by gentleness. You are weak and full of goodness." The alien face had no difficulty in conveying contempt. *"You are like the parents. You must be eliminated."*

The children stared silently at this confrontation. Kirk wondered if they were beginning to hear the hollow crack of breaking promises. They certainly looked as if the words of their "angel" were not quite what they had expected.

"Children," said Kirk suddenly, not taking his eyes off the alien, "I have some pictures of some of you on Triacus. I'd like to show them to you."

Tommy appeared to hesitate; it must have seemed an odd time for home movies. But events were moving too fast for him. The other children were frankly bewildered.

"Mr. Spock, the pictures."

"I forbid it!" said Gorgan.

"Why should you fear it?"

"I fear nothing!"

"So we were told. Mr. Spock, the children are waiting."

The film on the big screen showed Tommy and his father playing volleyball with the others. The remains of a picnic were strewn on the ground. Tommy stumbled and fell, and before he could decide whether or not to howl, his father had run to him and picked him up tenderly.

"There's me!" cried Mary. The children murmured as they recognized themselves.

The picture changed to the charnel house scene that

had met the *Enterprise* officers on Triacus. There was a collective gasp; then the graves and the inscriptions. Tommy rubbed his eyes. The little ones were very still.

"They would not help transport us. They were against us." Was the creature's voice acquiring a whine? *"They had to be eliminated."*

"Tommy's father would have destroyed you, but he recognized you too late," Spock stated flatly.

Gorgan rallied. *"You are also too late. The kind ones always are."*

"Not always. Not this time." Kirk looked at the children. Were those very bright eyes filling with tears at last? "You can't hide from them. They see you as you are. Even the children learn."

Gorgan summoned up an erratically brighter light around his cloaked body. He called to the children. *"You are my future generals. Together we will raise armies of followers. Go to your posts! Our first great victories are upon us! You will see, we have millions of followers on Marcos Twelve!"*

The children looked at the flickering figure with tear-blind eyes. The alien began to shout.

"We shall exterminate all who oppose us!"

"As you believe, so shall it be." As their belief waned, doubt began to creep as if it were an ugly bruise over the face of the "angels." The sweet false face was curdling.

"Don't be afraid," said Kirk. "Look at him!" McCoy was bending over the little group of sobbing children. The picture of the graves still hung on the screen. Tommy looked from the screen to the writhing alien, and back; he was holding his lower lip hard with his teeth.

"We must exterminate! Follow me!" Gorgan's head had erupted with hideous blotches.

"Without you, children, he is nothing," said Kirk. "He can no longer hide the evil Beast within himself."

"I command you, I command you . . ." the mel-

lifluous voice cracked and roughened. *". . . to your posts . . . carry out your duties, or I will destroy you. You too will be swept aside . . ."* quavered the dreadful thing in the shimmering cloak.

"How ugly he really is. Look at him, and don't be afraid." Kirk's hand was on Tommy's shoulder, which was shaking.

"Death, death, death to you all . . ." it died away in a scream of pure, weak anger.

McCoy looked up. "They're crying, Jim. They're finally crying! It's good to see."

Tommy was clinging to Kirk. He had broken down and was weeping convulsively. "M—my father—"

"It's all right, Tommy. It's all right. It is, isn't it, Bones?"

"Yes," replied the Doctor, picking up the nearest child. "We can help them now."

Trembling, Uhura raised her head and looked uncertainly at her console. She touched it wonderingly. But her attention was claimed by a very small nose being blown on her small skirt.

Sulu, in his own voice but sounding puzzled, said, "Marcos Twelve is dead ahead, sir."

"Reverse course, Mr. Sulu."

"Aye, aye, sir!" Slowly he reached for the controls, wary eyes on his screen.

"Course reversed!" he announced with triumph.

"Set a course for Starbase 4." How many times today had he given that order, Kirk wondered. It was good to see it obeyed.

He had command.

THE CORBOMITE MANEUVER
(Jerry Sohl)

Spock was making a map of the galaxy's planet systems, a long and tedious job. However, six of the nine squares of his screen were finally lighted on photographic charts of the star fields already explored by the *Enterprise*. His camera clicked again, and the seventh square broke into lighted life, picturing the quadrant of starry space through which the Starship was moving. Observant, Bailey, the newly appointed navigator, young, unseasoned, a novice in Starfleet service, eyed the square with clumsily concealed impatience.

"Three days of this, Mr. Spock. Other ships must have made star maps of *some* of this."

Spock spoke gently. "Negative, Lieutenant. We're the first to reach this far. We—"

He was interrupted by the siren shriek of the alarm; and Bailey, removing his eyes from Spock's screen, stared at the red light flashing on his own console. Leaning past him, Sulu called, "Sir! Contact with an object. It's moving toward us."

Spock rose, and, striding swiftly to the empty command chair, said, "Deflectors! Full intensity."

Half out of his chair, Bailey shouted, "And it's on *collision* course with us!"

"Evasive maneuvers, Mr. Sulu," Spock said mildly.

Working levers, Sulu took a reading of the results.

"Object's changing direction with us, sir. Keeps on coming at us."

Uhura's rich contralto spoke. "Getting no signal from it, sir."

"And it's still on collision course with us!"

The excitement in Bailey's voice contrasted only too vividly with the controlled, efficient composure of those of his bridge mates. Instead of registering the difference—and using it for improved self-discipline—he raised his voice to a near scream. *"And our deflectors aren't stopping it!"*

Spock said, "Sound general alarm. All hands prepare—"

Sulu broke in. "It's slowing down, sir."

The calm Vulcan voice said, "Countermand general alarm. All engines full stop."

"Visual contact!"

It was Bailey's cry undertoned by a triumph mingled with a now open arrogance.

As the *Enterprise* slowed to a stop, star movement halted with it. And on the bridge screen appeared a pinpoint of light that wasn't a star—an image which so swiftly expanded that the bridge's watchful eyes could identify it as a crystallike cube, rotating, luminescent and resuming its speed toward them. Then suddenly, it too stopped, hanging in space as it slowly revolved on its unseen axis, an eerie montage of unearthly colors changing, merging and dividing as the thing turned its faces toward them.

Spock looked away from it. "Ahead slow. Steer a course around it, Mr. Sulu."

But the moment they began to move, the cube moved with them.

"It's blocking the way!" Bailey roared. "Deliberately blocking it!"

Spock turned tranquil eyes on him.

"Quite unnecessary to raise your voice, Mr. Bailey. Unlike us, the object appears to lack hearing." Then addressing Sulu, he added, "Engines full stop. Sound the alert."

The stridency of the alarm shrilled again. Smacking buttons, Sulu said, "Bridge to all decks. Condition alert. Captain Kirk to the bridge!"

Kirk's well-muscled body was in shorts. McCoy had him lying on his back, arms pulling, legs pushing at an exercise device suspended from Sickbay's ceiling—a posture that hid the red light flashing over the door. McCoy noticed it; but absorbed in panel reports of Kirk's body functions, he decided not to mention it. It was his nightmare—persuading Kirk to submit to a medical exam. Yet monitoring the health of the elusive flea who was Captain of the *Enterprise* was his prime professional responsibility. Now was his rare, rare chance. And he didn't intend to lose it to the vagaries of electric lights—red, blue, yellow or any other color of the spectrum.

Completing his readings, he switched off the exercise machine and said, "Winded, Jim?"

Kirk slipped off the table. "If I were, you're the last person I'd tell—" and at the instant of speaking, registered the on-off flashing of the red light over the door. Racing to a panel, he switched it on and, pushing a knob, spoke into the intercom.

"Kirk here. What goes on?"

He learned.

The small screen over the intercom showed Spock's face, its moving lips. "Take a look at this, Captain."

Spock dissolved into a view of the slowly rotating cube. "Whatever it is," Spock's voice offered, "it's blocking our way. When we move, it moves too, sir."

Snapping the screen dark, Kirk grabbed up a sweatshirt, a towel; and shouldering head first into the sweatshirt, emerged from it to whirl on McCoy.

"You could see that light from where you were! Why didn't you say so?"

"At least I finished a physical on you, didn't I? What am I, a doctor . . ."

But Kirk was gone.

Gathering up his instruments, McCoy completed his

sentence to his own infinite reassurance and satisfaction. "... or a trolley car conductor? If I jumped every time a light blinked around here, I'd end up in a straightjacket."

Outside, Kirk, accelerating his pace, passed racing crewmen as Sulu's voice came over the loudspeaker.

"All decks alert. All hands to general quarters."

Kirk, tightening the towel around his neck, headed for the turbo-car elevator at the end of the corridor. The doors whooshed closed behind him and he said, "Bridge."

Relays whirred like crickets at the verbal instruction; and on the control panel, lights blinked as the car began its vertical ascent, the elevator hum growing with its increasing speed. But Kirk, chafing at the delay, pushed a button on the intercom panel.

"Kirk to bridge."

"Spock here, sir."

"Any changes?"

"Negative. Whatever it is, it seems to just want to hold us here."

"I'll stop to change, then." And shutting off the intercom, spoke to the turbo-car. "Captain's quarters."

Smoothly, the car braked; and when it resumed movement just as smoothly, altered its direction from vertical to horizontal.

In the bridge, Spock was standing beside Bailey, whose eyes seemed hypnotized by the indefinably sinister cube shown on the screen. Jerking the young navigator out of his trance, he said, "All decks have reported, Mr. Bailey."

Flushing, Bailey started.

"Yes, sir," he said, and rousing, turned off the still flashing red light on his console.

Spock, at his Vulcan coolest, said, "When the Captain arrives, he'll expect a report on—"

"—on the cube's range and position. I'll have them by then, sir."

As Spock gravely nodded, Bailey added, "Raising my voice back here, sir, didn't mean I was scared or

couldn't do my job. It just means that I happen to have
a human thing called an adrenalin gland."

Spock paused, startled by the aggression of this
backhanded reference to his alien origin. Then yet
more solemn-faced, he nodded again at Bailey.

"Sounds most inconvenient," he said. "Have you
ever thought of having it removed?"

He left Bailey for the command chair; and the red-
faced navigator, aware of a poorly muffled guffaw from
Sulu's station beside him, flushed still redder.

"Very funny," he sneered.

The choking Sulu recovered himself long enough to
say breathlessly, "Kid . . . you try to cross brains with
Spock—and he'll . . . cut you into pieces too small to
find."

"If I were the Captain—"

"He's even rougher. But I'm warning you, brother.
It comes as more of a shock because he's such a hell
of a leader."

The very rough Captain had opened his quarters
door to see his yeoman laying out one of his uniforms.
Unwinding the towel from his neck, he threw it at a
chair and said, "Thank you, Yeoman."

Apparently unruffled by his tone, Janice Rand said,
"Yes, sir," and opening the door, closed it behind her
as Kirk, yanking off his sweatshirt, shoved a switch
on a panel under a small screen. "Captain to bridge."

The screen lighted to the sight of his Science Officer's
face who said, "Spock here, sir."

"Any signs of life?"

"Negative, sir."

"Have you tried all hailing frequencies?"

"Affirmative. No answer from the cube."

Kirk pulled his uniform shirt into unwrinkled,
precise position. "Have the department heads meet me
on the bridge."

"Already standing by, Captain."

The cube was still revolving on its hypothetical
axis, its alternating, unnameable colors reflected from

the screen onto the human faces nearest it, making them unfamiliar. Tossing it a look, Kirk said, "Navigation?"

"Distance to us," Bailey said, "fifteen hundred meters, position constant."

"Helm?"

"Sir, each of its edges measures one hundred seven meters. Mass, a little under eleven thousand tons."

"Communications?"

"Hailing frequencies still open, sir," Uhura said. "No message."

"Mr. Spock?"

"Sensor shows it is solid, sir; but its principal substances are unknown to us."

"Engineering?"

"Motive power . . ." Scott shrugged. "A solid. Beats me what makes it go, sir."

Kirk smiled at him. "I'll buy speculation, Scotty."

"And I'd sell if I had any. How a solid cube can sense us coming, block us, move when we move . . . ah dinna ken, sir, as my people used to say. That's my report."

Kirk looked at McCoy. "Life Sciences?"

"Same report, Jim. No chance of life existing inside a solid cube; but there must be some kind of external intelligence somewhere directing it."

"Thank you, Bones."

Bailey exploded.

"We going to just let it hold us here, sir? We've got phaser weapons. I vote we blast it."

Kirk turned to look at him. When he spoke, his voice was dry as withered leaves. "I'll keep that in mind, Mr. Bailey, when this becomes a democracy."

He left his chair to move to the elevator, followed by other bridge people. Bailey, except for Sulu, was left standing alone beside his console.

"See what I mean?" Sulu said. "Sit down."

The enigmatic cube had held the Starship at bay for eighteen hours. Its origin, like its purpose, was still unknown to members of the exhausted crew, the eyes of Kirk, his officers and department heads bloodshot from study of star maps that consistently refused to show any habitable planet close enough to account for the mysterious object. In the Briefing Room, shoving aside the litter of graphs and computations on the table, he threw down his stylus and leaned back in his chair for a long stretch. Around him, others stifled yawns.

"Anything further, gentlemen?" Kirk said.

Spock spoke. "I believe it adds up to one of two possibilities. First, a space buoy of some kind—'flypaper,' sir."

The word so puzzled the others that it roused them. But Kirk, nodding at Spock, said, "And you don't recommend sticking around."

"Negative, Captain. It would make us look too weak."

Uhura voiced the general perplexity. "I thought I'd learned English by now."

Smiling, Kirk said, "Flypaper—a Nineteenth Century device—a paper Earth used to use covered with a sticky substance to trap insects which flew into it."

Scholarly, solemn, Spock said, "More your Twentieth Century, I believe, sir."

"Undoubtedly so, Mr. Spock," Kirk said.

"Somebody out there doesn't like us," Sulu said.

Kirk got to his feet, stretched again and sat down. "It's time for action, gentlemen. Mr. Bailey . . ."

The headlong navigator swung a lever on his table panel. "Briefing Room to phaser gun crews—"

"*Countermand!*" Kirk snapped, hitting a switch on his own panel. But his voice was unusually gentle as he addressed the now quaking Bailey. "Do you mind if *I* select the kind of action to be taken by my ship, Mr. Bailey?"

"I'm sorry, sir. I thought you meant—"

"Are you explaining, Mr. Bailey? When I want an explanation, I shall so inform you."

The navigator wilted. Kirk went on. "Now, as I

started to say, Mr. Bailey, plot us a spiral course away from the cube. Mr. Sulu, alert the Engine Room. We'll try pulling away from it."

Kirk rose and, at the Briefing Room door, waited until Sulu had pushed a panel button, saying, "Helmsman to Engine Room. Stand by, all decks alert. We're going to try pulling away."

In the bridge, a stricken Bailey punched in the spiral course and, without turning, said, "Course plotted and laid in, Captain."

From his chair, Kirk glanced around at his busy bridge crew. Then looking at the screened cube, said, "Engage, Mr. Sulu. Quarter speed."

Engine hum deepened; and as the *Enterprise* veered in its new curving course, stars slid sideways—but the cube kept exact pace with the ship.

"Still blocking us, sir," Sulu said.

"Then let's see if it'll give way. Ahead, half speed."

"Point five-o, sir," Sulu said.

With the increased speed, the cube loomed larger on the screen, rotating faster and its colors beginning to glow. Suddenly, warning lights burst into crimson on all control panels of the bridge, the cube now whirling dizzily, its colors growing in intensity.

Spock looked up from his mounded viewer. "Radiation, sir. From the short end of the spectrum. And its becoming stronger."

Kirk ordered the ship to a full stop. The stars came to a standstill. However, the cube, despite the *Enterprise's* stationary position, maintained its approach to the vessel, its colors flaring into violence.

"It's still coming at us!" Bailey said. "Range ninety meters, Captain."

His eyes on the screen, Kirk heard Spock say, "Radiation increasing, sir."

"Power astern, half speed, Mr. Sulu."

"Half speed, sir."

The engines' hum returned as they began to move the ship backward, the maneuver, instead of discouraging the cube's pursuit, inciting it to higher speed.

"Radiation nearing tolerance level, sir," Spock reported.

Revolving into blur now, the cube's brilliant colors were flooding the bridge with their reflections, distorting faces with gaunt shadows and inhuman skin shades.

"Still coming," Bailey said. "Gaining on us."

Kirk said, "Engines astern, full speed."

"Full speed, sir."

Stars sped away as the ship accelerated rearward, though the cube merely grew in size on the screen, its fiery glow still brighter as it twisted wildly on its axis.

"Range, seventy-one meters now, sir," Bailey said.

Kirk addressed Sulu. "Helm, give us Warp power."

Over the surge of Warp power added to the engine hum, Sulu said, "Warp One, sir."

Spock's voice was toneless. "Radiation at the tolerance level, Captain."

"Warp Two, sir," Sulu said.

The deadly, spinning top still clung to them; and looking at his Captain, Sulu said, "Speed is now Warp Three, sir."

"Radiation is passing tolerance level, Captain," Spock said. "Entering lethal zone."

"Range fifty meters and still closing!"

"Phaser crews stand ready," Kirk said.

"Phaser crews report ready, sir," Bailey said.

The stars were flying past in reversed movement as the cube, a blaze of viciously vivid colors, was closing the gap between it and the ship.

"Lock phasers on target," Kirk said.

Spock moved from his station to the command chair. "Radiation still growing. We can take only a few seconds more of it, sir."

Nearest the screen, they both had to shield their eyes from their pursuer's fierce glare.

"Phasers locked on target, sir," Bailey said. "Point blank range and closing."

"Fire main phasers."

The beams, striking the cube, exploded it, swamping the bridge in a blinding geyser of light. Then the blast waves hit, rocking the ship so that officers and crewmen had to grab at consoles to avoid being hurled to the deck. Bridge lights flickered, dimmed and the *Enterprise* hung motionless, a stilled, meaningless speck against the vast reaches of star-filled space.

Kirk, considering his phasers' removal of the blockage, felt no elation. Now what? To probe on ahead was only too probably to invite attack, its source as unknown as the attacker. Had the mysterious cube been an envoy of some murderous space-psychopath? Was he then to risk his ship and his crew—or turn back on his course? Restless, he joined Spock at his viewer.

"How do they describe our mission, Mr. Spock? Ah, yes. 'To go where no man has gone before.'"

"So it is said, Captain." The clear, straight eyes under the cocked brows met his. "However, sensors reveal nothing. No object, no contact in any direction."

"Care to speculate on what we'll find if we go ahead?"

"Speculate?" Spock shook his head. "I prefer logic, sir. We'll encounter the intelligence which sent the cube out."

"Intelligence simply different from ours—or superior?"

"Probably both. And if you're asking the logical decision to make—"

"I'm not."

Spock eyed him. "Has it occurred to you, sir, there is a certain inefficiency in questioning me about matters on which you've already made up your mind?"

"But it gives me emotional security," Kirk told him, deadpan. He turned. "Set course ahead, Mr. Bailey."

"Plotted and laid in, sir."

"Engage," Kirk said.

The engines whined up; and Sulu said, "Warp One, sir."

Now that decision for ongoing had been made, it called for some protective reinforcement. Back at his command post, Kirk looked at his bridge personnel, his face stern, uncompromising. "Navigator," he said, "Phaser crews were sluggish, and you were slow in locking them into your directional beams. Helmsman, Engineering decks could have moved faster too. Mr. Spock will program a series of simulated attacks and evasion maneuvers."

Focusing cold eyes on Bailey and Sulu, he said, "Keep repeating the exercises until I am satisfied, gentlemen."

McCoy had been standing at the elevator doors, watching and listening. Now as Kirk approached them, he spoke quietly. "Your timing is lousy, Jim. The men are tired."

"You're the one who says a little suffering is good for the soul."

"I never say that!"

As they stepped into the turbo-car, a look passed between them. McCoy *had* said it, would say it again —and they both knew it. He made no retort. Kirk said, "Captain's quarters," and the car began its descent as Bailey's voice came over its speaker. "This is the bridge. Engineering and Phaser decks, prepare for simulated attack. Repeat: simulated attack."

McCoy gestured to the speaking panel. "And I'm worried about Bailey. Navigator's position is rough enough on a seasoned man—"

Kirk's interruption was short and impatient. "I think he'll cut it."

"How so sure? Because you spotted something you liked in him . . . something familiar like yourself fifteen years ago?"

Irritated, Kirk was about to silence McCoy when he was silenced himself by Bailey's *"On the double,* deck five! Give me a green light!"

"Suppose you could have promoted him too fast? Listen to his voice, Jim . . ."

Once more Bailey's voice won McCoy a reprieve. "Condition alert . . . battle stations . . ."

The alert signal was still shrilling in the elevator when its doors opened on a corridor of running crew members, but Bailey's commands followed Kirk into his cabin. "Engineering deck five, report. Phaser crews, come on, let's get on with it!"

In a chair, eyes closed, drained and fatigued, Kirk listened. Clearly Bailey was enjoying the delegation of command. A kid playing with a terrible responsibility. As to himself, was he tired of it? Maybe. Choice, he thought, was an illusion. Untried and in moral darkness, one was impelled in a direction by unconscious forces beyond one's comprehension; by idealisms that turned out to be egotisms, a drive, for instance, not toward the harmonious music of the spheres, but to the glamor of a Starship command. And you were properly punished for such self-delusion by the absolute aloneness of command's heavy obligation.

"Here, Jim."

He took the drink McCoy handed him. "What's next? More humanism? 'They're not machines, Jim'?"

"They're—"

"I've heard you say that man is superior to any machines, Bones."

"I never said that either!" McCoy snapped.

At the flash of a red light on his cabin's panel, Kirk rose. "Kirk here."

Spock said, "Exercise rating, Captain. Ninety-four percent."

"Let's try for a hundred, Mr. Spock."

For the unflawed. Nothing less than human perfection could satisfy a Starship Captain. "I am tired," he thought. "I ought to be selling charter flights to Mars." And the door opened. Janice Rand, carrying a tray covered by a white cloth, bypassed Kirk and McCoy to place it on the desk beside the Captain's chair.

Kirk questioned her with frowning eyebrows.

Removing the cloth, she said, "It's past time you ate something, sir."

"What the devil? Green leaves? Am I a herbivore?"

The girl indicated McCoy. "Dietary salad, sir. Dr. McCoy changed your diet card. I thought you knew."

From the cabin's panel, Bailey said, "This is the

bridge. All decks prepare for better reaction time on second simulated attack."

Kirk, regarding the salad with loathing, picked up a fork, picked at it as Janice, a shade too professional, unfolded his napkin.

McCoy said, "Your weight was up a couple of pounds. Remember?"

Kirk, grabbing the napkin, threw it to the desk. "Will you stop hovering over me, Yeoman?"

"I just wanted to change it if it's not . . . all right, sir."

Kirk looked into the young, earnest, feminine gray eyes. A moment passed before he said, "It's . . . fine. Bring the doctor some too."

McCoy contemplated his feet. "No, thank you. I never eat until the crew eats."

Yeoman Rand poured some liquid into the glass on the tray.

Watching her, Kirk spread his left hand's fingers over his forehead and right eye. Politely he said, "All right, Yeoman. Thank you."

As she closed the door back of her, he closed his eyes. "Bones, when I find the Headquarters genius who assigned me a female yeoman—"

"She's very attractive. You don't trust yourself?"

He could, of course, Kirk thought, dash the glass of liquid into McCoy's face. That would quiet him down, discouraging transfer of his own male yens to other men who didn't feel them. But he was too tired to do a good job of it.

"I'm married," he said. "And a faithful husband. My girl is called the *Enterprise*. And the first mistake this other female, this yeoman makes—"

McCoy smiled, shaking his head. "She won't," he said.

Bailey spoke again from the cabin's panel. "Engineering decks alert. Phaser crews, let's—"

The alarm signal crushed his voice. Then as the panel's red light flashed on-off, Sulu, too controlled, said, interrupting, *"Countermand* that! All decks to battle stations! This is for real. Repeat. All decks to battle stations. *This is for real.*"

The red light on the panel buzzed.

Kirk said, "Kirk here."

Spock's filtered and uninflected voice said, "Sensors are picking up something ahead of us, Captain."

"Coming," Kirk said.

In the bridge, Spock, bent over his hooded viewer, lifted his head from it long enough to report to his Captain, "Exceptionally strong contact but not visual yet."

A silent Kirk watched him stoop again to appraise his dials and controls, and, frowning, punch in new coordinates. Their results inspected, Spock said tonelessly, "Distance spectograph . . . metallic, similar to cube . . . much greater energy reading."

Turning, Kirk said, "Screen on." But all it showed was stars arranged in a design which to human eyes was also random, undesigned. Then Sulu called, "There, sir!"

Kirk saw it too—a tiny speck of light already developing size even as he looked at it, a tightness beginning to constrict his chest as he said, "Half speed. Prepare for evasive action."

Sulu responded. "Reducing speed to Warp Two, sir."

The next moment, the *Enterprise* bridge seemed to upend, shuddering, twisting like a toy in the hand of a giant imbecile child. A guard at the door fell, sliding nearly the length of the deck before he caught hold of a cabinet handle. People grabbed at anything and everything that seemed to offer stability—their chair legs, console counters, steel files.

Spock, back in his seat, said, "Tractor beam, sir. It's got us—tight."

A recovered Sulu spoke. "Engines overloading, sir."

"All engines stop," Kirk said.

"All engines stopped, sir."

Kirk, resting his head against the back of the command chair, looked at the screen again where the light speck was magnifying into a shape.

"Object decelerating, sir," Bailey said.

At his library computer, Spock was getting results from his inputs. "Size and mass of the object—" he paused, shaking his head. "This must be wrong. I'm getting a faulty reading."

Kirk, resolving his conflict between his obsession with what the screen showed and his urge to ask Spock what he'd discovered about it, said, "Phaser crews stand by."

The thing on the screen had enlarged into a mass that should have made some identification of it possible; but like the cube, the image was too alien in appearance to make any judgment of it reliable. What it absurdly seemed to be was a rounded cluster of balls, each growing bigger as it neared. Curious and unbelieving, Kirk could see the cell-like sections pulsing with inner light.

As though to herself, Uhura whispered, "It's not true."

Spock, his eyes on the screen said, "No, I'm afraid my reading was accurate, sir."

The huge screen was rapidly becoming a formidable reporter. In the lower quadrant of its frame, the immense *Enterprise* hung motionless, and in the distance, the other ship (for it was a ship) was still small but was continuously growing. Soon it matched the size of the *Enterprise* in the opposite quadrant; but discontent with equality of mass, it increased its own, and went on increasing it until it was twice as large as the Starship, occupying the entire frame of the screen. When the alien vessel had completely dwarfed the *Enterprise*, it was so monstrous that only a part of it could be seen on the screen.

The bridge crew was stunned, struck down into awe as it contemplated the imaged Colossus. Spock alone regarded it with an interest as lively as it was intense.

Kirk spoke quietly. "Mass, Mr. Sulu."

The amazed Sulu said "Shooooosh!" Then registering Kirk's glance, added, "The reading goes off my scale, sir. It must be a mile in diameter."

Spock murmured, "Fascinating!"

"Reduce image," Kirk said.

Bailey was too dumbstruck to act, so Sulu, leaning across to his console, turned a switch. Gradually, the vastness of the screened shape diminished until the frame could hold it in its total form.

"Lieutenant Uhura, ship to ship," Kirk said.

"Hailing frequencies open, sir."

Kirk reached for his speaker. "This is the United Earth Ship *Enterprise*. We convey greetings and await your reply."

They were allowed to wait. Then Bailey, who had put on earphones, suddenly straightened. He froze, staring, his face blanched, his mouth slack and open.

"What is it, Mr. Bailey?"

The navigator turned his appalled face. "Message, sir . . . coming over my navigation beam." He swallowed, listened, clutching the earphones close to his head. Kirk looked away from him to address his Communications Officer.

"Pick it up, Lieutenant Uhura."

"Switching, sir."

The replay of the message, amplified, struck the bridge with an incoherent cataract of roar; but Kirk, joining Spock to listen, was finally able to discern words in what had been bedlam.

"*. . . and trespassed into our star systems. This is Balok, Commander of the Flagship Fesarius of the First Federation. . . . Your vessel, obviously the product of a primitive and savage civilization, having ignored a warning buoy of the First Federation, then destroyed it, has demonstrated that your intention is not peaceful . . .*"

The voice, issuing from a larynx of iron, paused before adding, "*We are now considering disposition of your ship and the life aboard.*"

"Ship to ship," Kirk said.

"Hailing frequencies open, sir."

Kirk, whose own voice, filtered, and amplified, sounded strange, spoke composedly. "This is the Captain of the U.S.S. *Enterprise*. The warning nature of your space buoy was unknown to us: our vessel was blocked by it and when we attempted to disengage—"

A squealing feedback, taking over, drowned his last sentence; and though Spock could see that his lips were still moving, only the squeal could be heard.

It stopped as Uhura, in obedience to a gesture from Kirk, cut the frequency. He stood silent beside Spock as the Vulcan's computer burst into a frenzy of red lights. Pulling at switches, twisting dials as though he were trying to shut something off, the Science Officer said, "Captain . . . we are being invaded by exceptionally strong sensor probes. Everywhere . . . our electrical systems . . . our engines . . . even our cabins and labs."

Amplified, the harsh voice of the Fesarius commander grated again throughout the bridge. *"No further communication will be accepted. If there is the slightest hostile move, your vessel will be destroyed immediately."*

Silence fell over the bridge personnel. Long experience in the unimaginable, training and self-discipline, though well indoctrinated, failed to rescue them from the paralysis induced by Balok's threat. Kirk was the first to move, walking to his command chair, aware as he'd been a thousand times before of his crew's eyes on him, hopeful, expectant, the miracle maker.

A couple of console lights faded and went dark. Spock, working at his panel, called, "They're shutting off some of our systems, sir. Brilliant! I'd like to study their methods."

As Kirk leaned forward in his chair, the humming of the bridge relays and servo-motors lost rhythm before going still.

"Mr. Spock," Kirk said, "does our recorder marker have all this on its tapes?"

"Enough to alert other ships, sir."

"Mr. Bailey, dispatch recorder marker."

Bailey merely stared at Kirk. Then as though the look in them had released him from some witchcraft, he made the proper adjustments on his panel; and wetting his dry lips, said, "Recorder marker ejected, sir."

"And it's on course," Spock said, lifting his head from his viewer. "Heading back the way we—"

White light flared from the screen, washing living faces with deathly pallor. Then another shock wave struck, tilting the Starship and once more compelling the bridge people to clutch at any available support. One hand outstretched to Sulu's console, the other hiding his eyes, Bailey whispered, "Oh, my God."

It was the moment Balok chose to make his deafening announcement. *"Your record marker has been destroyed."* Then came a second's reprieve before he added, *"You have been examined. Regretfully, your ship must be destroyed."*

Fury flamed in Kirk, a rage so violent that his knuckles whitened on his command chair's arms as he fought to pull it back to hitherto unknown deeps within himself. Vaguely, he heard Bailey give a sob.

The Fesarius commander was clearly enjoying his role of cat with mouse.

"Your ending will be painless. We make assumption you have a deity, or deities, or some such beliefs which comfort you. We therefore grant you ten Earth time periods known as minutes to make preparation. We will not alter our decision; we will not accept communication. Upon any evasive or hostile move, you will be instantly destroyed."

Kirk had won his struggle. The fury of rage had retreated to give way to a fury of thinking. Over at his station, Spock, working intently with his dials, said, "Might be interesting to see what they look like. If I can locate where that voice is coming from—"

Behind his command chair, the elevator doors must have opened, for McCoy and Scott hurried over to him, anxious inquiry in their faces.

"Jim . . . Balok . . . his message . . . it was heard all over the ship."

Someday, Kirk thought, I'll count up the ways used by my crew members to say to me, "Come on, Captain. You've got all the rabbits in the hat. We need one now. Pull it out." And the truth was, he *had* pulled many out. Oh, yes, there'd been the defeats—the failures to establish the bond of a common life between him and an alien race—yet, more often, he had succeeded in creating the sense of shared life. And those of his crew who hadn't seen him do it had been told about it.

So he had something going for him. Yet this was a hard one. Where did you find the right words for people with ten minutes to live, healthy young people denied the gradual, benevolent sense debilities with which age prepared one for the eternal stillness—sightlessness, deafness, unawareness of touch?

"Jim . . ." McCoy said again.

Nodding, he hit his intercom switch.

"Captain to crew."

And speaking, said the words that had come to him, perhaps from the same deeps whence his rage had come.

"Those who have served for long on this vessel have encountered apparently inimical and alien life forms. So they know that the greatest danger facing us is . . . ourselves and our irrational fear of the unknown. . . ."

In his own ears, his voice sounded firm and steady. Why? He went on.

"But there is no such thing as the unknown. There are only things temporarily hidden, temporarily not understood—and therefore temporarily feared. In most cases, we have found that an intelligence capable of a civilization is capable of comprehending peaceful gestures. Certainly, a life form advanced enough for space travel is advanced enough to eventually recognize our motives. All decks stand by. Captain out."

As he turned, he saw that Uhura's lustrous black eyes were tear-filled.

If to one of his people he had made sense, it was enough.

"Ship to ship, Lieutenant Uhura."

"Hailing frequencies open, sir."

Reaching for his speaker, he said, "This is the Captain of the *Enterprise*. We came here seeking friendship and have no wish to trespass. To demonstrate our goodwill, our vessel will return the way it came. But if attacked—"

Once more the squealing feedback killed his voice; and once more he motioned for cut of the circuit.

"Mr. Bailey, lay in a course away."

"What? . . . Course? What . . . ?"

Sulu leaned past the shaken Bailey to move a couple of levers on his console.

"Course plotted and laid in, sir."

"Engage, Mr. Sulu. Warp Factor One."

"Warp Factor—" Sulu began, and, frantically working his own controls, wheeled to Kirk.

"There's no response, Captain!"

"Switch to impulse!"

"All engine systems show dead, sir. And weapon systems."

Spock called, "Switching to screen, sir! I think I can get something visual."

He achieved it.

On the screen, the star background began to ripple like a sea flecked by plankton's phosphorescence. Then it dissolved into a still rippling but gradually firming shape—the distorted yet fairly distinct image of what could only have been Balok. The creature's long, drooping face was set in what seemed to be a permanently grotesque grimace, the nostrils of his bulbous nose upturned to expose blood-red flesh, a space-clown out of nightmare. As to his eyes, they explained the cat-mouse game—green balls, thrust out, black-slitted.

The thick lips moved.

"You are wasting time and effort. There is no escape. You have eight Earth minutes left."

The picture, wavering, blanked out.

Spock's tone was that of an astronomy professor explaining "black holes" to a classroom of freshmen. "I was curious to see how they appeared, sir."

God bless Spock, Kirk thought, almost smiling. "Yes, of course you were."

Bailey, lurching to his feet, screamed.

"I don't understand this at all! Spock's wasting time —everyone else just hangs around! *Somebody's got to do something!*"

McCoy went to him quickly. "Easy, boy, easy."

"What do they want from us, Doctor? Let's find out what they want us to *do!*"

Kirk's casual tone was all the more impressive for its unimpressedness.

"They want us to lose our heads, Mr. Bailey. Don't accommodate them."

"We've only got eight minutes left!"

Sulu said, "Seven and forty-one seconds."

Bailey spun, his eyes following Sulu's to the clock on the helmsman's instrument panel. Set to count off minutes and seconds, the minute hand held to "seven" while the second hand moved from "39" to "38" to "37."

Bailey, pointing to the dial, shrieked, *"He's doing a countdown!"*

McCoy seized the navigator's arm. "Practically the end of your watch. Why don't—"

Bailey jerked free, almost throwing McCoy to the deck.

"Are you all out of your heads? End of *watch? It's the end of everything!"*

Kirk said, *"Mr. Bailey."*

It was a voice he seldom called upon because it cost too much—the paradoxes of compassion and impersonal authority . . . of ignorance masquerading as wisdom, of self-possession wavering toward randomness.

Bailey flailed free of McCoy. "What are you, *robots*? Wound-up toys? Don't you know when you're dying? Watches and regulations and orders—what do they mean when—?"

"You're relieved, Mr. Bailey," Kirk said.

Bailey, swinging toward Kirk, started to shout a reply which, at the look on his Captain's face, emerged as a groan. The effort to control himself left him shaking.

Kirk spoke to McCoy. "Escort him to his quarters, Doctor."

Bailey strode off to the elevator alone, McCoy running after him. Kirk's eyes left its closing doors, returning to the screen.

"Lieutenant Uhura, ship to ship."

"Hailing frequencies open, sir."

"This is the Captain of the Earth Ship *Enterprise*. However, it is the custom of Earth people to make every effort—"

The feedback squeal overwhelmed his words once more; but this time, Kirk made no gesture to cut off the circuit. There'd been enough bullying. If you knew what your intentions were—and they were peaceful—you gave them voice, undeterred by interruption. That was self-respect: standing by your truth. Unimaginably, the squeal ended, and Kirk, his voice calm despite the hope suddenly buoyant in him, resumed his communication to the commander of the Fesarius.

"—to avoid misunderstanding with others. We destroyed your space buoy in a simple act of self-preservation. When we attempted to move away from it, it emitted radiation harmful to our species."

No response.

Kirk went on. "If you have examined our ship and its tapes, you know this to be true."

The squeal screamed and then was gone, exiting like a bit player in a theater, making deferential way for the star's reappearance. On the screen, Balok's monstrous face wavered into focus. Its mouth said, *"You now have seven minutes left."*

The hot rage burned in Kirk again.

He couldn't afford it, not with the despair, the expectation of that new rabbit out of the hat on the faces around him. Anger like this was a weakness, not beautiful, but just a fierce resentment at one's failure to exert control, power—and the resultant hate of helplessness to do it. Waste all your vitality in resistance to factual helplessness; and what you did was to cripple the resourcefulness you needed to devise some way out of it. Yet it was trust of his resourcefulness alone that was supporting his people's courage in the face of death.

"Four minutes, thirty seconds," Sulu said.

Scott blew up. "You have a inappropriate fascination with time pieces, Sulu!"

Sulu shrugged, and Kirk, leaving his command chair, went to Spock. "What's the matter with them? They must know by now that we mean them no harm."

There was balm in the quiet, dark eyes. Half-smiling, his best friend said, "They are certainly aware by now that we are incapable of it, sir."

From the screen, Balok said, *"Four minutes."*

Kirk looked away from it. "There has to be something to do! Something I've overlooked!"

Under the calm in Spock's voice, there was respect, affection—no demand for rabbits. "In chess," he said conversationally, "when one is outmatched, checkmate. The game is over."

It was safe to explode with Spock. "Is that your best recommendation? Accept it?"

Spock, realist and friend, said, "I regret that I can find no other logical one, sir."

McCoy appeared beside them. "Assuming we find a way out of this—"

"Nobody's given up yet!" Kirk snapped.

McCoy's tone changed. "Then on Bailey. Let me put it in my medical records as 'simple fatigue.'"

"That's *my* decision, Doctor!" Kirk said.

Turning, he crossed over to his command position,

his hand on its chair back, abstracted, wrenching at his brain for some answer.

And McCoy, following him, said, "And it was *your* mistake. Expected too much, pushed him, over-worked—"

Kirk's fist clenched. *"I'm ordering you to drop it, McCoy. I've no time for you, your buck-passing theories or your sentimentality!"*

McCoy was not subdued.

"Assuming we get out of this, Captain, I intend to challenge your action in my medical records. I'll state I warned you about his condition. And that's no bluff."

"Any time you can bluff me, Doctor—"

At once Kirk was aware that he himself had cracked a bit under the suspense and strain, and conscious too that his raised voice had made him an object of surprised dismay by the bridge personnel. He had increased fear instead of allaying it. Well, there was nothing to do about it. He'd just have to trust to their experience of him.

Harsh, guttural, Balok said, *"Three minutes."*

Kirk, his self-possession recovered, ignored the warning to speak to McCoy. "Fine, Doctor. Let's hope we'll be able to argue it through."

Nodding, McCoy moved off, and Kirk, his hand shielding his closed eyes, suddenly removed it and, rising from his command chair, went to Spock.

"Not chess, Mr. Spock. *Poker!* Do you know the game?"

Instead of waiting for the Vulcan's answer, he walked back to his chair, the idea that had come to him putting out fronds of hope and encouragement, developing, growing. And was no longer disturbed by the eyes focused on him, waiting, waiting for that rabbit of magic.

"Lieutenant Uhura, ship to ship!"

"Hailing frequencies open, sir."

Kirk sat upright. "This is the Captain of the *Enterprise. . . .*"

He paused, his voice steady. "Our respect for other

126

life forms requires that we now give you this warning. There is one critical item of information never committed to the memory banks of any Earth Ship . . ."

Half-aware of Sulu's astonished face, he continued. "Since the early days of space travel, our vessels have incorporated into them a substance known as corbomite. It is a material formed into a device which prevents attack on us." He voice deepened, not to threat but into uninflected impressiveness. "If any destructive energy form touches our vessels, a reverse reaction of equal strength is created, destroying—"

Interrupting, Balok said, *"You now have two minutes."*

Spock left his position to come and stand quietly beside Kirk, who went on as imperturbably as though the palms of his hands on his chair arms weren't wet with sweat.

"—destroying the attacker. It will interest you to know that since the initial use of corbomite more than two of our centuries ago, no attacking ship has ever survived the attempt. Death has little meaning for us. If it has none for you, then attack us now. We grow annoyed at your foolishness."

At his nod to Uhura, she clicked off the circuit.

"Well played, sir," Spock said. "I believe it was known as a 'bluff.' I regret not having learned more about this . . . Balok." He gestured toward the screen. "Some aspects of his face reminded me of my father."

Scott spoke. "Then may Heaven have helped your mother."

"She considered herself a most fortunate Earth woman," Spock told him coolly.

McCoy moved toward them and Kirk said quietly, "I'm sorry, Bones, I—"

"For having other things on your mind?" He smiled. "My fault. My timing was out—"

"One minute," Balok said, not echoed, but in precise unison with Sulu who'd been checking his instruments by the half-second. Catching Scott's glare, the helmsman shrugged, addressing Kirk.

"I knew he would, sir."

Kirk laughed. "Has it ever occurred to you you're not a very inscrutable Oriental, Mr. Sulu?"

Turning, Sulu grinned. "I tried it once when I was a kid. Remember those old . . ." he halted, searching for the word . . . "images on celluloid stuff?"

"Cinema," Kirk said.

"Movies," Scott offered.

"Yes, cinema," Sulu said. "The ones about the time of the Sino-Western trouble . . ."

Uhura spoke. "World War III, almost."

Nodding, Kirk said, "The world was lucky it was stopped in time. None of us here would be enjoying life today . . ." As he noticed McCoy's grin, his words trailed off into a silence broken by Sulu.

"Well, anyway, the villains were Oriental, remember? I loved them. I used to sit in front of the mirror for hours practicing drooping eyelids, mysterious expressions. I never knew what it meant. These movies were two hundred years old, I guess, but I wanted to be like them."

Turning, Uhura smiled at him. "You never made it."

"I can't figure out why I'm like this. I don't have a *drop* of Western blood."

A heavy silence flowed in over the bridge, all the heavier for its contrast with Sulu's lighthearted comments; but the general anxiety was too present to continue idle conversation. Sulu had turned back to his timepiece when the elevator doors opened and Bailey stepped out, his face defensive and uncertain.

"If anyone's interested," Sulu said, ". . . *thirty* seconds."

McCoy had seen Bailey at the bridge's rear, and Kirk, registering the constraint in his face, turned and saw the navigator too. Bailey approached the command chair briskly.

"Sir, request permission to take my post."

As Kirk eyed him, Sulu said, "Twenty seconds, Captain."

There was a brief pause before Kirk said, "Permission granted, Mr. Bailey."

He looked away as Bailey resumed his seat beside Sulu and his console's instrument clock, ticking off its "zero" seconds.

"Ten," Sulu counted, ". . . nine . . . eight . . . seven . . ."

Spock, almost too quiet-faced, had returned from his position to stand beside his Captain.

Sulu said, ". . . six . . . five . . . four . . . three . . . two . . . one . . ."

The zero count passed; and as nothing happened, Spock spoke.

"An interesting game, this 'poker.' "

Kirk nodded. "It does seem to have advantages over chess."

Balok's voice, filtered and grating, said, *"This is the Commander of the Fesarius."* But as Uhura leaned forward to throw her hailing-frequency switch, Kirk stopped her with a gesture.

"Hold on, Lieutenant. Let's let him sweat for a change."

A minute passed before Balok said, *"The destruction of your vessel has been delayed."*

"You gotta admire him," Sulu said. "The latest news every minute."

Somebody laughed a little too loudly, the sound of the relieved guffaw followed at once by Balok's voice.

"We must have proof of your corbomite device."

Spock strode back to his station, beginning to manipulate controls as Balok went on: *"We will relent in your destruction only if we have proof of your corbomite device. Do you understand?"*

Kirk waited four minutes by Sulu's clock before commanding the opening of hailing frequencies.

"Request denied," he said.

"You will be destroyed unless you give us this information."

Spock, gesturing toward the screen, said, "Captain—"

Again the hideous image of Balok assumed its wavering shape. And the voice said, *"And now, having permitted your primitive efforts to see my form, I trust it has pleased your curiosity."* The balled eyes moved slightly. *"What's more, another demonstration of our superiority . . ."*

To a click, the *Enterprise* viewing screen went dark and the Fesarius Commander added, *"We will soon inform you of our decision regarding your vessel."*

Kirk was leaning back, stretching in a weariness induced by the accumulation of strains when Yeoman Janice Rand walked through the opened elevator doors, carrying a tray of coffee and cups. As nonchalant as though the bridge were her personal drawing room, she set down the tray and was immediately surrounded by a group of men, including McCoy.

"I thought the power was off in the galley," he said.

Pouring the steaming brew into cups, she said, "I used a hand phaser. Zap! hot coffee!"

She started off with a filled cup for Kirk, and Sulu cried, "Something's going on, Captain!"

Kirk made a swift, rejecting gesture toward the coffee, he and Spock both concentrating on the ship's viewing screen.

Indeed something was going on. A small, cell-like section of the Fesarius was separating itself from its mother ship and moving away from it but still remaining visible within the screen's frame. Spock lifted his head from his hooded viewer, saying, "Weight—about two thousand metric tons, sir."

"Yes, it appears to be a small ship."

The small, balled alien ship had moved nearer to the *Enterprise;* and as it approached still closer, its mother ship sped off, its cell-like sections dwindling rapidly in size. Accelerating fast, the thing lost shape to speed, turned to a pinpoint of light, then into a nothingness that left the tiny ship hanging before the *Enterprise.*

Balok's voice, filtered, spoke.

"It has been decided that I will conduct you to a

planet of the First Federation which is capable of sustaining your life form."

Kirk, a man of action, gave vent to the frustration imposed upon him by many hours of inaction by slamming his clenched fist on his command chair's arm. Near him, Sulu, leaning back in his chair, gazed up at the bridge deck ceiling, whistling a "Musetta's Waltz," which was still played on old Earth tapes of the Puccini opera. Beside him, Bailey stared at the dials on his console.

As to Balok, he went on.

"There you will disembark and be interned. Your ship will be destroyed, of course."

To nobody in particular, Kirk muttered, "Of course," though at bridge stations around him, lights were blinking on. And from across the room, Spock called, "Engine systems coming on, Captain."

But Balok's sense of comedy was as grotesque as the snouted face. Filtered, the thick voice said, *"Do not be deceived by the size of this pilot vessel. It has an equal potential to destroy your ship."* And as if to give proof of the claimed power, the *Enterprise* was subjected to a jolt that sent several people sprawling.

Spock said, "Tractor beam again, sir."

Kirk went very still as the voice, going on, pushed home the point.

"Escape is impossible. It is only that you may sustain your gravity and atmosphere that your systems are now open. Our power will lead you to your destination. Any move to elude me or destroy my ship will result in the instant destruction of the Enterprise *and of every life aboard her."*

For some reason he preferred not to examine, Kirk wanted to smile. There, on the viewing screen, was Balok's tiny ship towing the huge *Enterprise* behind it across the dark fields of star-sown space. It *was* absurd, and the portentous pomposity of Balok himself, his literary style, gigantically threatening, made it still more absurd.

But to his not-amused people, he said, "Our plan:

131

A show of resignation. His tractor beam is a heavy drain on his small ship. Question: Will he grow careless?"

Bailey, gesturing toward his console, said, "Captain, he's pulling out a little ahead of us."

Spock, to check the report, emerged from his hooded viewer to announce, "He's sneaked power down a bit."

Kirk, turning, confronted a white-faced, tense Bailey who spoke hastily, "I'm all right, sir."

Nodding, Kirk said, "We'll need a right-angle course to maintain our sheer away from him no matter how he turns."

"Yes, sir."

"Maximum acceleration when I give the word."

Sulu, his eyes on the screen, said, "Yes, sir."

Minutes which everyone endured according to his duties and temperament crawled sluggishly by. Bailey constantly ran his tongue over dry lips. Sulu kept his eyes on his Captain. As to Spock, expressionless, he waited, alert as a drawn trigger.

Kirk, without turning, spoke to Sulu. *"Engage!"*

Under the prearranged pressures of switches and controls, the bridge lights dimmed to a massive power drain as the *Enterprise* lurched, shuddering. And on the screen, Balok's dwarf ship lurched too, its light beginning to pulsate. And started to flicker in power surges as it tried to compensate for the withdrawal of the *Enterprise*.

It wasn't so simple as it should have been. The Starship's engines rose to a higher and higher whine until Sulu unnecessarily reported, "It's a strain, Captain. Engines are overloading."

"More power," Kirk said.

He caught a glint of awed respect in Sulu's eyes. And wondered what the response would be if he said, "Cut it, kid." If I've taken a risk, it's because I'm alive. Living itself is a risk. If you don't want to risk, phaser yourself and die. And thought, I am as bored by excessive dependency as I am by excessive awe.

Spock, bless him, was neither dependent nor awed. Now without intonation, he said, "We're overheating, Captain. Intermix temperature seven thousand four hundred degrees ... seven-five ... seven-six ..."

When the alarm bell rang, he shut it off. "Eight thousand degrees, sir."

On the screen, Balok's ship was glowing like a nova as it tried to fend off the pull of the *Enterprise* in their titanic tug-of-war.

The bridge teetered, rocking, as the *Enterprise* tried to pull free of Balok's ship, the whine of its engines growing to a scream.

Kirk, hard-jawed, said, "Sheer away, Mr. Bailey!"

His brow sweating, Bailey battled the power conflict. And from his station, Spock said, "We're two thousand above maximum. Eight thousand four ... five ... six ... she'll blow soon."

Even as he was speaking, the light pulsations from Balok's ship lessened. Then one of the lights flickered into dimness.

"We're breaking free, sir," Bailey reported.

All the lights on the alien ship became faint. As one blinked off and then on again,. there came a sudden flare-up of brilliant light from the balled vessel to be replaced by an utter darkness. And the *Enterprise,* freed, sped away into the distance.

A relaxed Kirk, leaning back in his chair, said, "All engines stop."

"All stopped, sir," Sulu said.

Turning, Kirk studied the young face of Bailey. Its blue eyes met his straightforwardly. Nodding, he said, "Good. All hands, good."

Behind him, the elevator doors opened, and Scott, his face anxious, almost ran to the command chair. "Engines need some work, Captain! They've been badly overstrained. Bad. Can we hold it here a few hours?"

Spock left his station to take his own place beside the command chair. "If Balok got a signal through to that mother ship of his, sir ..."

Kirk, nodding, said, "Right, Mr. Spock. We're not home yet."

Uhura, swinging her chair around, bent her head to a turned switch on her console. "A signal, Captain . . . very weak." For several seconds, she just listened. Then she said, "It's Balok, sir, a distress signal to the Fesarius. His engines are out . . . his life-sustaining system isn't operating. He's repeating the message to the Fesarius."

"Any reply, Lieutenant?"

"Negative, sir. His signal is fading. It is so faint, I doubt if the mother ship could hear it."

On the screen before Kirk, there hung Balok's little ball, once so charged with belligerent vitality but now helpless, dull—a black nothing against the star-strewn immensities of space. And about it was something of pathos, of miniscule tragedy like the disappearance down a whale's throat of the microscopic, one-celled lives inhabiting the seas.

"Plot a course for it, Mr. Bailey," he said.

Only Spock among his officers showed no surprise, not even the lift of a astonished eyebrow. Kirk, pushing his intercom button, reached for his mike to say, "This is the Captain speaking. The First Federation vessel is in distress. We're preparing to board."

His crew had been persecuted by Balok, overworked, threatened, panicked. So the right words had to be found to explain the suggestion of mercy in his announcement; and choosing them, he went on: "There are lives at stake. By our standards 'alien lives'—but still lives. Captain out."

Navigator Bailey, doing his best to keep the respectful awe out of his eyes said, "Course plotted and laid in, sir."

"Ready the Transporter Room, Mr. Scott."

After a moment's hesitation, Scott said, "Aye, sir," and walked toward the elevator as Kirk, turning to Sulu, said, "Bring us to within one hundred meters, Mr. Sulu. Ahead slow."

Sighing, Sulu repeated the order and Kirk, glancing

around him, saw that the still lingering dissatisfaction on the faces of his people was telling him that more right words were needed. He rose from his chair and, grasping its back, said, "Gentlemen, what is the mission of this vessel of ours? It is to seek out and make contact with life forms wherever we find them." He stopped, and, wheeling, pointed to the dark round little ship on the screen. *"Life,"* he said, and after a long pause, hammered home his point. "An opportunity to demonstrate what our high-sounding words mean. Any questions?"

As nobody spoke, he went on.

"I'll take two men with me. Dr. McCoy to examine and treat the aliens if possible." He was at the elevator doors when he turned. "And you, Mr. Bailey."

Astounded, Bailey managed a "Sir?"

"The face of the unknown, Mr. Bailey. I think I owe you a look at it."

Rising slowly from his seat, Bailey said, "Yes, sir."

Spock had left his place too. "Request permission, sir, to—"

"Denied, Mr. Spock. If I'm mistaken, if Balok's set a trap for us, I want you here."

With Bailey, McCoy joined Kirk in the elevator, his medical bag in his hand. And to Kirk's "Transporter Room," the familiar relays clicked, lights flashing. After a moment, Kirk addressed McCoy, ignoring Bailey's fear-paled face. "You don't approve either, I suppose."

McCoy shrugged. "I never ask your approval of my diagnoses."

"Frightened, Mr. Bailey?" Kirk said.

"Yes, sir."

"Of what?"

"Well, as far as knowing exactly—"

"Precisely my point, Mr. Bailey."

As the trio entered the Transporter Room, Scott, an assistant beside him, looked up from the transporter controls to warn, "It will be risky, sir. We're locked in on what appears to be a main deck."

Nodding, Kirk said, "Air sample?"

"Breathable, Captain. In fact, a slightly higher oxygen content than our own."

"Ready, Doctor?" Kirk asked, turning to McCoy.

"No, but you won't let that stop you."

Bailey, last to enter the transport chamber, obediently stepped into the space Kirk indicated; and from the console across the Room, Scott, motioning them all to stoop, called, "On your hunkers, Captain. It reads pretty cramped over there."

Kirk, satisfied that he and his companions were safely placed, said, *"Energize!"*

With the hum of increasing power, the three dissolved into unidentifiable figures of light sparkles, the transporter effect subsiding as they disappeared only to almost immediately materialize under a ceiling barely an inch above their heads. Around them was a subdued, soft lighting, probably indirect, but no sign whatever of smoke or trouble.

Then still bending, the three stopped dead, dumbstruck by the luxury of the room before them. The floor was covered by a rich, deep-piled form of carpet, its gold color matched by draperies of what might have been velvet but wasn't. In the room's center, on a silver and jade-green chaise longue, a creature reclined. Was it Balok? The head was even larger than it had shown on the *Enterprise* screen, and its body had a curious limpness about it.

It didn't move as they approached it. The goggle eyes in the huge, bloated head had no lids to blink but simply stared glassily at the opposite wall. When McCoy tapped the thing with his knuckles, it gave out a hollow sound; and nodding, McCoy said, "Jim, this is a . . . a dummy, a puppet of some kind."

And the familiar harshness of Balok's voice said, *"I have been waiting for you."*

At the sound of it, whey all wheeled.

Kirk's first thought was, "I'm hallucinating." For the actual Balok was almost a child in size, less than four feet tall, chubby, warm and so cuddly in appearance that one could only marvel how his pudgy chest could accommodate the resonance of that voice. Smiling cherubically so that his rosy cheeks made little mounds under his twinkling eyes, he was sitting relaxedly in a small chair, robed in some shimmering turquoise material—anyway, some color of the blue-green family.

"I'm Balok," he said. "Welcome aboard."

Moving forward, Kirk let the phenomenon of the voice go to watch the childlike hand indicate three small armless chairs.

"I'm Captain Kirk. I—"

Interrupting, their host nodded. "—and McCoy and Bailey. Sit. Be comfortable."

As the *Enterprise* men lowered themselves gingerly to the edges of what by Earth standards would be children's chairs, Balok pushed a button on the wall beside him. It slid open to make way for a servo unit bearing a bowl and four cups. Lifting a ladle, Balok dipped it into the bowl to fill the cups of his hospitality.

"We must drink. This is tranya. I hope you relish it as much as I."

"Commander Balok—" Kirk began, and was stilled by a wave of the little hand.

"I know. I know," the voice grated. "A thousand questions. But first, the tranya."

Midget though he was, this creature had deflected the *Enterprise* in its course, demoralized its crew with terrorizing threats and made a general nuisance of himself. Kirk accepted the cup he was handed but didn't drink. Nor did McCoy. Balok beamed at them. Lifting his own drink, he sipped from it. After a moment, Kirk and McCoy followed his example, Bailey, still uneasy and distrustful, preferring to merely hold his drink.

The tranya was delicious, but as Kirk replaced his empty cup on the servo, his eyes veered to the chaise longue where the enormous, hideous head lolled idiotically, half-on and half-off its cushion.

Noticing, Balok said, "My alter ego, so to speak,

Captain. In your culture, he would be Mr. Hyde to my Jekyll. You must admit he's effective. You would never have been frightened by me. I also thought my distress signal quite clever." And with another seraphic smile, Balok added, "It was a pleasure testing you."

Eyeing the manikin, Kirk said, "I see."

Balok spoke earnestly. "I had to discover your real intentions, you see."

"But you probed our memory banks . . ."

"Your records could have been a deception on your part." As Balok spoke, he poured more tranya into his cup, offering to pour more for Kirk who declined. McCoy, however, accepted more drink, asking, "And your crew, Commander?"

Balok giggled. "Crew? I have no crew, Doctor. Just Mr. Hyde and me. I run everything from this small ship." The heavy voice became unexpectedly plaintive, the chubby face wistful. "But I miss company, conversation. Even an alien would be a welcome companion. Perhaps one of your men . . . for some period of time . . . an exchange of information, cultures . . ."

The contrast between the powerful voice and its ingenuous confession of loneliness was appealing. Kirk was finding much to like in Balok and a considerable degree of sympathy for him, marooned here alone in space with the bogeyman puppet on the chaise longue.

"Yes," he said. "Do you think we can find a volunteer, Mr. Bailey?"

Bailey jumped from his child's chair with such enthusiasm that he hit his head on the ceiling.

"Me, sir!" he cried eagerly. "I'd like to volunteer!"

Kirk waited a long moment before he nodded, saying, "An excellent idea, Mr. Bailey."

Unbelieving, Balok stared at the *Enterprise* navigator. "You will stay with me? Be my friend? You represent Earth's best, then?"

Rubbing his head, Bailey protested. "No, sir. I'm not. I'll make plenty of mistakes."

"And you'll learn more about us this way, Commander Balok," Kirk said. "As to me, I'll get back a better officer in return."

Balok broke into open, joyous laughter so infectious that Kirk laughed too.

"I see, Captain," he said. "We think much alike, you and I."

Bailey, the decision made, swallowed his whole drink of tranya.

As he finished it, Balok got to his small height; and moving grandly to the door, stood at it, waiting for his guests to join him. He looked up at them, towering over him, his face that of a child on Christmas morning. The next minute, he was all business again.

"Now, before I bring back the Fesarius, let me show you my personal vessel. It is not often I have this pleasure."

McCoy, following him through the door, shook his head with the wonder of it all, but Kirk and Bailey smiled at each other before they too stooped to move through the entranceway in the trail of robed childman.

Pausing at another small door, Balok, turning, said "Yes, we're very much alike, Captain. Both proud of our ships."

SHORE LEAVE
(Theodore Sturgeon)

Captain James Kirk slumped in his chair and contemplated his viewscreen. At least this planet was not emitting torpedoes or mysterious signals, for once. He sincerely hoped it wouldn't start anything; he wasn't at all sure he could deal with another Problem. Even his mind felt sluggish.

He became vaguely aware of footsteps nearing him; he couldn't allow himself to slouch like this. He straightened up with effort and felt a stab of pain in his back.

"Anything from the landing party yet, Mr. Spock?"

"They should be sending up a report momentarily, Captain." Spock glanced at him. "Is something wrong?"

"Kink in my back. Yes, just about there."

A strong hand touched, assessed and began to knead the spastic muscle. He could always rely on Spock.

"Just a little higher. Ohh—yes. Just there, Spock. Harder—push hard . . ." But Spock was standing in front of him.

"What—?" Her hands skillfully working, Yeoman Tonia Barrows smiled as he turned his head. He couldn't start using the female crew as personal masseuses. Damn. "Thank you, Yeoman," he said hastily. "That's sufficient." It had helped.

"You need sleep, Captain," said the girl hesitantly. "If it's not out of line to suggest—"

"I've had enough of that from Dr. McCoy. Thank you."

Spock folded his arms. "And Dr. McCoy is completely correct, Captain. After what this crew has been through in the last few months, there's not a man aboard who doesn't need a rest."

"Myself excepted, of course."

Sometimes, Spock was almost insufferable. But Kirk didn't really have to remain on the bridge just now; he could be doing the ship's log from his be— . . . quarters, while he waited for the landing party to report.

He fumbled the switch to "Record": "Captain's Log, Star Date Three-Oh-Two-Five point uh . . . three," he said wearily. "We are orbiting an inun—unan—uninhabited planet in the Omicron Delta Region. A planet remarkably like Earth—or how we remember Earth. Prelinimary—preliminary reports make it sound too good to be true: flowers and trees, very restful." He yawned. "Pending the report from the scouts, I plan to authorize a snore—shore leave. . . ."

Downstairs, the landing party was gratefully inhaling fresh air scented with herbs and flowers. Tall trees rustled gently in a light breeze. The sky was cornflower blue. How long since anyone aboard the *Enterprise* had had a chance to even notice weather, undistracted? McCoy wondered.

There were no buildings; just the trees. No beings but themselves and the daisies; and the quiet. They never noticed the constant sounds of the ship's systems until they were not there.

"It's beautiful," said Sulu, gazing at the forests and green meadows. "No animals, no people, no worries . . . just what the doctor ordered, right, Doctor?"

"I couldn't have prescribed better," said McCoy happily. "We are one weary ship."

"Do you think the Captain will give us shore leave here?"

"Depends on my report, and those of the other scouts," said McCoy. "Oh!" He stopped short.

Sulu followed his look. Ahead of them, a small lake lay like a jewel in a setting of emerald leaves. Flowering shrubs covered the banks, and a willow wept gracefully into the water.

"You have to see this place to believe it," said Mc-Coy with great delight. "It's like something out of . . . *Alice in Wonderland!* The Captain has to come down here!"

Sulu nodded in total agreement. "He'd like it."

"He *needs* it. You have your problems, and I have mine. He has his, plus ours plus those of four hundred and thirty other people." McCoy drifted toward the water, soaking up sun and warm air. Rapt in his wonderland, he barely remembered to look back at Sulu. "What are you doing?"

Sulu was crouched over a plant, adjusting his tricorder. "Getting cell structure records—a blade of grass, a bush, a flower petal; with these, we can analyze the whole planet's biology."

McCoy left him to it. He wasn't feeling at all analytical. He wandered down a faint path, absorbing peace, and wondering.

"Oh! My paws and whiskers! I shall be late!"

McCoy came to with a bang. Aural hallucinations, he diagnosed. He himself must be more tired than he had thought. Paws and whiskers, indeed. He turned very slowly.

There it was. Running on twinkling hind feet. About four feet tall with white fur and long ears, pulling an old-fashioned turnip watch from its waistcoat pocket.

"Tch!" The white rabbit disappeared through a gap in the dense shrubbery.

McCoy shook his head. I didn't see that. I am quite, quite sure that I didn't see that, he told himself. The bushes behind him rustled.

"Excuse me, sir," said the little girl in the pinafore,

politely. "Have you seen a rawther large white Rabbit with a yellow wais'c't and white gloves hereabouts?"

McCoy did not believe this either, of course. But in a stunned trance, he pointed after the rabbit.

The little girl curtseyed and said, "Thank you veddy much," and disappeared after the rabbit.

McCoy closed his eyes tight. "Sulu! SULU!"

He wasn't going to look anymore. Let Sulu see things. He, McCoy, was not obliged to believe any impossible things *after* breakfast.

"What is it? What's the matter?"

"Did—did you see them?"

"See what? I don't see anything," said Sulu, looking around. "What is it, Doctor?"

McCoy gulped. "I—uh—" There was nothing to say. He followed Sulu helplessly..

"Captain?"

Somebody at the door. Wake up. Alert. Responsible. Blood, start circulating. You can do better than this. "Yes?"

"Spock, Captain. I have the doctor's report on the crew."

"Come in, Spock." Kirk dragged himself together and stood.

"All systems are now on automatic, Captain, and skeleton standby crew is ready to relieve the bridge, Communications and Engineering." Spock was very businesslike.

"We'll beam the starboard section down first, Mr. Spock. Which party would you like to go down with?"

"Unnecessary in my case, Captain. On my planet, to rest is to *rest,* to cease using energy. To me, it is illogical to run up and down on green grass, using energy instead of saving it."

Insufferable.

The desk communicator sounded. "Kirk here."

"Dr. McCoy is calling from the planet, sir."

"Good. Open a channel, Lieutenant Uhura."

"Captain," said McCoy. "Are you beaming down?"

"I hadn't planned to, Bones. Why?"

"Well," said McCoy, "either our scouting probes and detectors are malfunctioning, and all of us scouts getting careless and beauty-intoxicated, or I have to report myself unfit for duty."

"Explain." Kirk quelled a wave of depression. A Problem. Either malfunctioning equipment or a malfunctioning staff. Great.

"On this supposedly uninhabited planet," McCoy stated with great precision, "I just saw a large white rabbit pull a gold watch out of his vest pocket. Then he claimed he was late."

Kirk burst out with relieved laughter. Not a Problem after all. "That's very good, Bones. Now I have one for you. The rabbit was followed by a little blonde girl, right?"

"Er . . .," said McCoy. "As a matter of fact, she was . . . and they disappeared through a hole in the hedge!"

Still chuckling, Kirk said, "I'll take your report under consideration, Doctor. Captain out." He turned to the baffled Spock. "That was a McCoy-pill, with a little mystery sugarcoating. He's trying to get me down there. But I won't swallow it."

"Very well, Captain," said Spock. "There was something I came to discuss." Kirk looked at him. "I picked this up from Dr. McCoy's log."

At last Kirk observed that Spock was holding a paper.

" 'We have a crew member who shows signs of stress and fatigue. Reaction time down nine to twelve percent. Associational rating norm minus three.' "

Concern penetrated the fog of Kirk's exhaustion. "That's much too low a rating," he said sharply.

" 'He is becoming irritable, inefficient, and quarrelsome. And yet he refuses to take rest and rehabilitation.' " Spock looked up. "He has the right, of course, but—"

"A crewman's rights end where the safety of the ship begins. That man will go ashore on my orders," said Kirk with annoyance. "What's his name?"

"James Kirk."

His head jerked up. That's what comes of giving orders before you have all the details. Inefficient. And they'd caught him fair and square.

Spock handed him the paper. "Enjoy yourself, Captain. It's an interesting planet. I believe you'll find it quite pleasant, very much like your Earth. The scouts have detected no life forms, artifacts or force fields of any kind; nothing but peace and sunlight and good air. You'll have no problems."

Kirk shrugged and finally smiled. "You win, Spock. I'll go."

Yeoman Barrows accompanied him down, and they materialized near two of the scouts.

"Rodriguez, Teller," Kirk acknowledged. "Everything all right?"

"Yes, sir," replied the dark boy, who was packing up a box of samples. "We've completed the specimen survey." The ensign with him was looking just a little wistful. Perhaps she was too tired to work.

"Sufficient, Mr. Rodriguez. Beam your reports up to Mr. Spock, and start enjoying yourselves."

The girl brightened. "Yes, sir!" said Rodriguez, handing her the tricorder. "Oh, sir, I think you'll find Dr. McCoy just over there."

Kirk looked "there," and all around him. "Restful here, isn't it? After what we've gone through, it's hard to believe a planet this beautiful exists."

"It is beautiful." The yeoman in the brief skirt twirled around. "So lovely and peaceful and—" she caught herself on the edge of burbling. "Oh, I mean— affirmative, Captain."

Kirk allowed himself a small smile at her youthful bounce, and he started toward McCoy with Yeoman Barrows. "McCoy? Where are you?"

The foliage was thick in this glade. "Over here!"

McCoy was still standing where he had seen what he had seen.

"Bones! Know any good rabbit jokes lately?" The doctor was not going to live that down for some time.

"Matter of fact, I do," said McCoy. His expression was too serious for comfort. "But this is not one of them. Look at this."

Kirk's smile faded as he followed McCoy's pointing finger. Tracks. On a planet without animals. Big tracks, in pairs. A hopping creature.

"I saw what I saw, Jim. Maybe I hallucinated it. But take a look here and tell me what you think."

"Aren't those prints kind of big for a rabbit?"

"Er—" McCoy looked a little sheepish. "As I reported, Captain, this was a most unusual rabbit."

Kirk dropped to his knees to study the footprints. "I admit I thought it was a joke. But these tracks are very real." The prints were far apart. It must have had long legs. A large hopping creature. "What about Sulu? Will he confirm what you saw?"

McCoy shook his head. "He was examining the flora at the time."

"I don't like this, Bones." Kirk flipped open his communicator. "Bridge. This is the Captain. Has the first shore party beamed down yet?"

"Negative, Captain. They're just about to start."

"Give them this message. Stand by. No one is to leave the ship until you hear further from me."

There was a brief delay before Uhura's voice came back with a dejected, "Aye, aye, sir."

McCoy protested. "Are you canceling the shore leave, Jim?"

"Until we find an explanation of *this*." He pointed at the enigmatic tracks.

"But the crew, they badly need rest."

"I know." said Kirk, feeling the weight of responsibility very heavily indeed. "But what you saw looked harmless. It probably is harmless, but before I bring my people down, I want proof that it is harmless."

McCoy was about to object that the worst that could happen would be an encounter with a pack of cards, when he was interrupted.

Shots. Gunshots.

So much for peace and tranquility; Kirk drew his phaser and started running. He stopped short as he found Sulu standing in a clearing, grinning happily and aiming at an innocent leaf.

Bang!

McCoy caught up with Kirk as he was saying wearily, "Mr. Sulu, what do you think you're doing?"

"Target shooting, Captain," said Sulu. "Isn't it a beauty? I don't have anything like this in my collection!"

"Where did you get it?"

"I *found* it. I know it's a crazy coincidence, but I've always wanted one. I found it lying right back there." He held it out proudly for Kirk's inspection. "An old-time Police Special, and in beautiful condition. Hasn't been a gun like this made in, oh, a couple of centuries. Look, it fires lead pellets propelled by expanding gases from a chemical explosion."

Sulu and his hobbies. "I've seen them before," said Kirk, remembering certain adventures when he had tangled with Earth's past history. He took the weapon and smiled at Sulu. One couldn't blame him, but—"I'll hang on to it. This fresh air seems to have made you a little trigger-happy."

Sulu looked disappointed but said only, "Yes, sir."

Yeoman Tonia Barrows was not interested in guns. As soon as she had seen that they were not confronted with an emergency, she had begun to wander. Now she called. "Sir! Dr. McCoy's rabbit. He must have come through here."

She pointed at a set of tracks, identical to the first, that crossed the clearing into the wood beyond.

Kirk examined the tracks. "Bones, are you certain your instruments showed no animal life on this planet?"

"Absolutely. No mammals, birds, insects, nothing.

I'm certain our readings weren't off, and yet . . ." He stared down at the perplexing prints.

Kirk sighed. "I'd like to believe this is an elaborate gag. But—" He stood up and looked toward the wood. "Yeoman Barrows, you accompany Mr. Sulu. Find out where those tracks come from." The pair turned to the shrubbery. "You come with me back to the glade, Doctor. I want another look at that area."

As they began walking back to the aquamarine lake, Kirk said with some bitterness, "This is becoming one very unusual shore leave."

McCoy said lightly, "It could be worse."

"How?"

"*You* could have seen that rabbit."

Kirk laughed in spite of his worry. "What's the matter, Bones? Getting a persecution complex?"

"I'm starting to feel a little bit picked on, if that's what you mean," said McCoy ruefully.

"I know that feeling well. I had it at the Academy." They strolled on. McCoy noted with satisfaction that Kirk seemed a little less tense. "An upperclassman there—one practical joke after another, and always on me. My own personal devil, a guy by the name of Finnegan."

"And you, being a serious young cadet—?"

"Serious? Bones, I'll make a confession. I was absolutely *grim*. Which delighted Finnegan. He was the one to put a bowl of cold soup in your bed, a bucket of water propped on a half-open door. You never knew where he'd strike next."

McCoy thought, "And you're still sore about it, long past as it is."

"More tracks, Bones. Looks like your rabbit came from over there." McCoy stooped and looked at the ground. "A girl's footprints too, Jim. The blonde girl I saw chasing it."

"Bones, you follow the rabbit. I'll backtrack the girl. We'll meet on the other side of that hill." McCoy nodded. Kirk started walking along the line of small boot-prints. Little girls, rabbits, old-fashioned guns—whatever next?

He hadn't thought about that lout Finnegan in years. What a thorn in his flesh that man had been! He remembered the day . . .

Tall, broad-shouldered, with a challenging grin pasted on his map, a figure was waiting by the tree in front of him. Kirk blinked. *"Finnegan!"*

The youth, dressed in Academy cadet uniform, swaggered up to him with a wicked laugh.

"Never know when I'm going to strike, eh, Jimmy boy?" The same faint brogue, the same cackling derision. As Kirk stood there, incredulous, he was jarred into accepting this reality by a sudden right to the jaw which knocked him flat. He got up slowly, staring at his old enemy who danced in a fighter's crouch, baiting him. "All right, Jimmy boy, go ahead. Lay one on me! Go ahead; that's what you've always wanted, isn't it?" It was. Kirk let go his disbelief and crouched. He was not going to pass up this chance to deal with this old bête-noire at last. Red rage surged in him as he remembered all the bullying, the merciless persecution.

"Come on, come on!" sneered Finnegan. Kirk started at him.

"Let's do that one again!"

A woman screamed. Oh, hell. And he pulled his punch. Yeoman Barrows? He was the Captain. His yeoman was in danger. Hell. He ran toward the sound of the scream, with Finnegan calling after him, "Any excuse, Jim baby? Right? Run away, that's right!"

McCoy appeared from the underbrush, running.

"What was that?"

"Barrows. Come on."

They found the girl huddled against a tree. Her tunic was torn and her hair disheveled. She was alone and weeping hysterically.

"What happened?"

"I—I—I don't know. I mean—I do know," she

sobbed. "I guess . . . I was following those tracks and . . . ohhh! There he was!"

"There who was?" snapped Kirk. This was no way for a trained crewman to give information.

"Him!" wailed the yeoman.

"Barrows, give me a report!"

She began to gain control of herself. "He had a cloak, sir. And—and a dagger with jewels on the handle."

McCoy was examining her. "Yeoman Barrows, are you sure you didn't imagine this?"

She pulled up the torn shoulder of her dress, suddenly embarrassed. "Captain, I know it sounds incredible." The men nodded. "But I didn't imagine it anymore than I imagined he did this." She gestured with the ripped tunic.

"All right," said McCoy reassuringly. "We believe you. But who was your Don Juan, anyway?"

"How did you know?" she gasped.

"Know what?"

"It was so, you know, sort of—storybook, walking around this place." She sniffed, and went on rather shyly. "I was thinking, all a girl needs here is Don Juan. Just daydreaming. You know?" She looked at the officers hesitantly. "Like you might think of some girl you'd like to meet."

Kirk was not prepared to dwell on this. He looked around, missing something.

"Mr. Sulu was with you. Where is he?"

"Oh. He ran after . . . him. He—" But Sulu was nowhere in sight.

"Stay with her, Doctor." Kirk took off at a run.

"Mr. Sulu!" he called. "Sulu! Where are you?" There was no reply. He brushed through the undergrowth and into a clearing; here was a miniature desert-garden, with cactus flowers blooming. Still calling, he began searching among the rocks.

There were footsteps on his right. "Sulu?"

It was not Sulu. The young girl smiled, real roses

on her dress stirring in the breeze. She came toward Kirk with memory in her eyes.

"Ruth." The memory kindled in the Captain. "You! How—I don't understand—"

"Jim, darling. It is me. It's Ruth." He had clamped that particular wound closed, forever. Somehow in the pressure of final examinations and qualifications and his first cruise, he had lost her, and put away the regrets.

"You don't think I'm real." He had even forgotten the gentleness of her voice. It all came flooding back with pain and longing. "But I am, darling, I am."

James Kirk's Ruth could not possibly exist here and now. But as she put her soft arms around his neck, he did not doubt her reality. He could not help but return her embrace.

He tried to resist; he took out his communicator. "Dr. McCoy, come in." But his eyes were fixed on Ruth. "McCoy, do you read me?"

She put the communicator to one side. "Think of nothing at all, darling, except our being together again." Her soft hair brushed his face.

"Ruth. How can it be you? You can't be here!"

She snuggled closer and looked up at him, her skin glowing in the sun. "It doesn't matter. Does it?"

Fifteen years ago. She still looked exactly the same, the fresh, young, gentle creature who had wept so bitterly at their last goodbye. She said again, "It doesn't matter. None of that matters, Jimmy."

His communicator beeped, cutting through his daze.

"Kirk here."

McCoy wanted to know if he had found Sulu.

"What?" She still wore her hair in a coronet of braids.

"Did you find Mr. Sulu?"

"Oh—no," said Kirk absently. "But I'm sure he's all right." She was dreaming into his eyes. "I mean, why shouldn't he be?"

"Captain, are *you* all right?"

"Oh, yes, I'm fine." The communicator seemed to float away by itself to the rock beside him. It beeped again.

He sighed, and acknowledged. "Yes, Mr. Rodriguez."

"Captain, a while ago, I saw . . . well, birds. Whole flocks of them."

"Don't you like birds, Mr. Rodriguez?" She was holding his hand in their special clasp.

"I like them fine, sir. But all our surveys showed—"

Kirk hadn't noticed the bird song that was coming from the forest. It had seemed to belong there.

"Offhand, Mr. Rodriguez, I'd say our instruments must be defective." It didn't really seem to matter. "There are indeed life forms on this planet." She nestled against his shoulder.

Rodriguez was being stubborn. "Sir, our survey couldn't have been that wrong."

Ruth moved a little away from him and regarded him with longing.

"Rodriguez, have all search parties rendezvous at the glade. I want some answers to all this."

"Aye, aye, sir." He couldn't let it happen again, lose her again. Nor could he abandon his crew to whatever dangers this mysterious planet held. Yearning and duty fought in his belly.

Ruth held out her hand to him and gave him a radiant smile. "You have to go."

"I don't want to." How he didn't want to!

This time, she did not weep. She bent toward him and said gently, "You'll see me again—if you want to." She kissed his cheek and backed away from him. He started after her.

"But I have to ask you— You haven't told me—"

"Do what you have to do. Then I'll be waiting, Jim." Would she? This time? He called her as she vanished into the wood. The communicator beeped again.

"Captain Kirk here." His eyes were still fixed on the gap between the trees where she had disappeared.

Mr. Spock said, "Captain, I am getting strange readings from the planet's surface. There seems to be a power field of some kind down there now."

"Specify."

"A highly sophisticated type of energy, Captain, which seems to have begun operating since we took our original readings. It is draining our power aboard ship and increasingly affecting communications."

"Can you pinpoint the source?" Kirk's attention was now reluctantly engaged.

"It could be beneath the planet's surface, but I cannot locate it precisely. Its patterns would indicate some sort of industrial activity."

Industrial activity? Here among the woods and fields? "Keep me posted, Mr. Spock. We'll continue our investigations from down here."

Investigations were proceeding slowly. Dr. McCoy sat with Yeoman Barrows under the birch tree. She was still clutching her torn tunic to her shoulder.

"Feeling better?"

She smiled. "A little. But I wouldn't want to be alone here."

"Why not?" McCoy gave a long, contented sigh. "It's a beautiful place. A little strange, I admit, but—"

"That's just it. It's almost too beautiful. I was thinking, before my tunic was even . . . torn, in a place like this, a girl should be dressed to match." Yeoman Barrows was showing an unsuspected streak of romanticism. "Let's see now . . . like a fairy-tale princess, with lots of floaty stuff and a tall pointed hat with a veil."

McCoy looked down at her kindly. Then he looked again. She was really a lovely young woman. Funny he had never noticed before. Of course, she had been a patient.

She was really *very* pretty.

"I see what you mean. But then you'd have whole armies of Don Juans to fight off." She chuckled. "And me too."

She glanced up from lowered eyelids. "Is that a promise, Doctor?"

They began walking around the lake. The twittering of birds filled the air, and the greenness of leaves burnished with sunlight filled their eyes.

"Oh!" On a bush, a heap of fabric was carelessly flung. White silks fluttered. "Oh, Doctor, they're lovely!" Yeoman Barrows picked up a stream of veiling.

"Yes, they are," agreed McCoy, looking at Yeoman Barrows's bright eyes.

She covered her face and peered at him over the veil. "Look at me!" She pirouetted lightly, and then promenaded, and spoke with mock seriousness. "A lady to be protected and fought for, a princess of the blood royal!"

What had taken him so long? "You are all of those things, and many more." He must have forgotten how to play, with all the heavy preoccupations of his work. Bless her, she had not. She was gay and vulnerable and lovely.

He took the costume from the shrub and pushed it into her arms. "They'd look even lovelier with you wearing them."

Her impish look changed suddenly to terror as she looked back at the bush. "Doctor, I'm afraid."

"Easy now," he said comfortingly as she buried her face in his shoulder. He could feel her trembling. He tried not to notice that her tunic had fallen from her shoulder. He felt a momentary stab of jealousy of that tedious "Don Juan" who had seen her first. "Look, I don't know what, or where or how, but the dress is here." He smiled down at her. "I'd like to see you in it."

She looked at the clothes doubtfully as she disengaged herself. She held the dress up in front of her; in spite of her qualms, she was obviously tempted. He nodded encouragement. She said, "All—all right!" and stepped around the bush. "But you stay right there— and don't peek!"

"My dear girl, I'm a doctor," said McCoy with dignity. "When I peek, it's in the line of duty."

Leonard McCoy, gentleman medic, found himself unable to avoid noticing the flinging of a tunic and the tantalizing motions that showed over the top of the shrubbery. His communicator sounded.

"Calling Dr. McCoy, come in please, Calling—"

He raised the instrument to his ear. "McCoy here." What a time for a call. And the voice was very faint. "I can't read you very well. Is that Rodriguez?"

"This is all the volume I get on this thing. Can't read you very well either. Captain's orders. Rendezvous at the glade where he first found you."

"Right. Rodriguez? What the devil's wrong with the communicators? Esteban? Esteban!"

McCoy shook the instrument as if it were an old-time thermometer, and then shook his head and shrugged. As he turned back for a last peek, he gasped.

Yeoman Barrows was gone. In her place stood a medieval vision, clad in a tall pointed hat and a pale green dress that clung to her body and spread in graceful folds below her hips. Her face was aglow, and she wore her veil like a bride.

Why the hell hadn't he noticed?

The Captain was consulting his Science Officer. He could barely hear.

"I want an explanation, Spock. First, there's Alice in Wonderland when there was supposedly no animal life. Then Sulu's gun, where there were no refined metals. Then the birds, and my—the two people I saw."

"Is there any chance these could be hallucinations, Captain?"

"One 'hallucination' flattened me with a clout on the jaw. The other—"

"That sounds like painful reality, Captain."

"And then there are the tracks . . ."

"There has to be a logical explanation. Captain, your signal is very weak. Can you turn up the gain?"

"I'm already on maximum."

There was a pause. "Captain, shall I beam down an armed party?"

Kirk thought not. "Our people here are armed with phasers. Besides, there's yet to be any real danger. It's just . . . Captain out." He stood for a moment, watching the sudden flight of a flock of birds across the sky. He was still so very tired. If only this shore leave could *be* a shore leave instead of an enigma! Why were those birds in the air? Something must have startled them. Sulu! He was still unaccounted for. Kirk rubbed his eyes and started into the forest.

There was a faint scream, shouting and thuds. As he ran, Kirk called to McCoy. Sulu burst out of the wood at top speed.

"Take cover, Captain! There's a samurai after me!"

"A what?"

No one, nothing was following Sulu, who stopped and looked over his shoulder, panting. "A samurai. With a sword—you know, an ancient warrior. Captain, you've got to believe me!"

"I do," said Kirk. He couldn't doubt Sulu. "I've met some interesting personalities here myself. Have you seen the rest of the landing party?"

"Rodriguez called a few minutes ago. Just before I met the samurai. He said you were rendezvousing back at the glade."

They started moving toward the meeting point, Sulu glancing nervously behind him.

"I hope Rodriguez got through to everybody. Communications are almost out."

"That's not all," said Sulu. "I tried to take a shot at the samurai. My phaser's out." He shoved the useless weapon back into his belt.

Kirk was still holding his own, drawn as he had heard the sounds of Sulu's encounter. He pointed it at the ground and fired. Nothing happened. He checked the settings and fired again. Slowly he replaced it in his belt.

"We had better get to the glade," he said grimly.

"Yes, sir. We— Look!"

The air was shimmering. A familiar shimmer, but erratic and uncertain. "Someone's beaming down from the ship."

Someone was certainly trying to, but there appeared to be some obstruction.

Willing the transporter to operate, as if that would do any good, Kirk waited. The shimmer faded, erupted, faded; with one last splash of sparkles, Spock materialized in front of them.

"Spock! My orders were no one was to leave the ship."

"It was necessary, Captain. I could not contact you by communicator, and the transporter is almost useless now. As I told you, there is an unusual power field down here. It seems to be soaking up all kinds of energy at the source. I calculated the rate at which it was growing, and reasoned that we might be able to transport one more person." Spock conveyed, with a lift of his eyebrow, that while white rabbits and such were beyond his comprehension, unexplained force fields were not to be tolerated. "We barely managed that."

Kirk had to approve this decision. "Good. I can use your help."

Sulu said anxiously, "We're stranded down here, Captain?"

"Until we find out what this is all about."

A tiger roared in the distance.

"That way!" said Kirk. "Spread out, find it." He tried not to think about the ineffective phasers.

At the glade, Tonia Barrows and McCoy looked for the others a bit reluctantly.

"There's no one here."

"This is the rendezvous point," said McCoy. The

girl wandered around the clearing. The doctor followed her slowly. "What was that? I thought—I swear I heard something."

"Don't talk like that!" In spite of the splendid costume and the warm eyes of McCoy, she was still jumpy.

"A princess shouldn't be afraid, not with her brave knight to protect her." Tonia managed a small smile and moved nearer to the shelter of a sun-warmed oak.

"Aaah!" There was a wild flurry of black and white—she was struggling with someone. McCoy ran.

The plumed hat was jaunty; pointed beard, jeweled doublet, swirling cloak. McCoy sailed in, fists flying. The cowardly lecher couldn't fight. Don Juan slunk off.

McCoy held her for a moment as she pulled her gown back together and straightened the tall hat, feeling extremely chivalrous. He had battled for his lady, and he'd do it again.

Hoofbeats sounded in the distance. They whirled, and saw, across the meadow, a gigantic horse emerging from the wood. The horse reared and wheeled as its rider perceived them.

McCoy's belief was strained almost to breaking point. The Black Knight lowered a wicked-looking lance and charged.

These fairy-tale characters were interrupting him too often. McCoy had had enough. He was going to deal with this apparition on the proper terms. A figment of the imagination was not real, could do no harm. He was not going to react anymore to hallucinations. He stepped out, unarmed, and confronted the oncoming menace, concentrating on denying the evidence of his senses.

The great black animal pounded across the meadow, the lance couchant.

"Look out, Bones!" McCoy ignored Kirk's cry of warning. Steadily, stubbornly he marched directly toward the galloping rider.

Kirk's phaser failed. He scrambled the old-fashioned pistol that he had confiscated from Sulu from his belt, as the wicked lance took McCoy through the chest.

The horse reared as Tonia Barrows screamed, and the Black Knight bent to retrieve his weapon. Kirk fired rapidly, and the armored horseman crashed to the ground a few yards away. Tonia's shrieks rose shrilly amid the echoes.

She fell to her knees over the prostrate McCoy. "He's dead, he's dead. It's all my fault. It never would have happened ... Ohhh!"

"No, Tonia——" said Kirk.

"But it was, it was. My fault. I am to blame!" She was screaming and weeping. "I've killed him, I've killed Leonard." Kirk took her arm, but she wrenched away from him and beat her fists on the ground.

"Yeoman," said Kirk in his sternest voice. "We're in trouble. I need every crewman alert and thinking."

The hysteria left her cries. "Yes, sir." Struggling for composure, she rose slowly to her feet.

Spock covered McCoy's body, hiding the gaping wound. Kirk turned away for a moment. He could not quite control his face. His friend was dead. Shore leave. And they were all looking to him for strength. He schooled his expression to a rocklike calm, and without looking back, strode purposefully toward Sulu. Sulu was crouching over the body of the Black Knight.

"Captain," he said worriedly, "I don't get this."

"Neither do I, Mr. Sulu," said Kirk, staring down with hatred at the sable armor. "But before we leave this planet, I *will*."

"Then you'd better have a look at this, sir." Sulu opened the visor and revealed the face of McCoy's murderer.

"What the——?" Perfectly molded skin, straight nose, regular as a waxwork, the mask stared back at him.

"It's like a dummy, Captain. It couldn't be alive."

"Tricorder?"

"Barely operating, sir."

"Spock!" Kirk handed the instrument to the First Officer. "What do you make of this?"

Spock took readings with some difficulty. "This is not human skin tissue, sir. More resembles the cellular casting we use for wound repairs. Much finer, of course."

"Mr. Spock!" Kirk stood up. "I want an exact judgment."

"Definitely a mechanical contrivance. Its tissues resemble the basic cell structure of the plants here—the trees, even the grass—"

Kirk peered at the face again. "Are you suggesting that this is a *plant,* Spock?"

Spock indicated extreme puzzlement by a slight frown. "I'm saying all these things are multicellular castings. The plants, the people, the animals—they're all being manufactured."

"By who? and why?" said Kirk blankly. "And why these particular things?"

Spock shook his head. "All we know for sure is that they act exactly like the real thing. Just as pleasant —or just as deadly."

Esteban Rodriguez had not yet had a chance to report his encounter with the Bengal tiger, which had leaped from the rocks and snarled at him. He had managed to get away, and was telling Yeoman Angela Teller about that and other things as they headed for the glade.

There was a buzzing sound. They looked around, and finally up. Overhead, a Sopwith Camel banked and dipped.

"What is *that?*"

"Of all the crazy things. Remember what I was telling you a little while ago about the early wars in the air, and the funny little vehicles they used?" Angela nodded, looking up at the sky. "Well, that's one of them."

The plane veered back and looped over their heads. Angela eyed it dubiously. "Can it hurt us?"

"Not unless it makes a strafing run." Rodriguez was rather pleased. No one could have asked for a better opportunity to show off his special knowledge. He had never expected to see one of those planes actually flying!

"A what?" She was impressed, he could tell.

"The way they used to attack people on the ground," he said offhandedly.

The biplane's engines roared as it banked and started toward them. It dived. The rat-tat-tat of vintage gunnery tore the air to shreds.

"Santa Maria!" Rodriguez dragged the girl toward the shelter of the nearby rocks. As the plane zoomed away, she dropped.

"Angela!" He lifted her. Her head lolled unnaturally limp, and her weight was dead in his arms.

Kirk and Spock were staring at the distant aircraft when Sulu called them.

The bodies of McCoy and the Black Knight had vanished.

"Look," said Sulu. "They've been dragged away."

They were stranded in a nightmare. "Mr. Spock!" said Kirk desperately.

The Vulcan was uncomfortable. "At this point, Captain, my analysis may not sound very scientific."

"McCoy's death is a scientific fact." The one undeniable reality.

"There is one faint possibility. Very unlikely, but nevertheless— Captain, what were your thoughts just before you encountered the people you met here?"

Kirk tried to remember. "I was thinking about . . . the Academy."

"Hey, Jim baby!"

There he was again. Finnegan. Lolling against a tree across the glade.

"I see you had to bring up reinforcements," he sneered. "Well, I'm still waiting for you, Jim boy!"

Maybe. "Finnegan! What's been happening to my people?"

The cadet, characteristically unhelpful, snickered and ducked back among the trees. His mocking laughter floated back to Kirk, who gritted his teeth.

"Take Mr. Sulu. Find McCoy's body. This man's my problem." He started across the glade.

"Captain—" Spock began.

"That's an order, Mr. Spock!" Kirk plunged into the trees in Finnegan's wake.

The laughter penetrated the forest. Kirk stalked after it. But it came from the left, and then the right, and straight ahead.

"This way, Jim boy, that's the boy."

He rounded a clump of trees and came on a bare rocky hill. No grass grew here; it was wild and deserted—except for the derisive voice.

"Old legs givin' out, Jimmy boy? Ha-ha-heeheehee!"

The voice came from behind him. He whirled, and it came again from above.

"Just like it used to be, Jim boy, remember? You never could find your head with both hands."

Kirk clenched his fists. He was going to get even with Finnegan if it was the last thing he did.

On a spur to his right, Finnegan called, "Over here, Jimmy boy!"

"Finnegan! I want some answers!"

"Coming up! Ha-ha-hee!" Kirk pursued the elusive voice until he was seething with fury; at last Finnegan stayed long enough on a rock above him for Kirk to start climbing.

With practiced ease, Finnegan met him in a violent bulldogging roll. They fell together to the flat ground and Kirk was briefly aware of a profound satisfaction —at last it had come to a clinch. Finnegan had never lost a fight; you could feel that in his confidence and skill, and Kirk took the impact of blow after blow without being able to land a really good punch. And he was winded from the chase.

Finnegan stood up and looked down at him. "Get up, get up. Always fight fair, don't you, you officer-and-gentleman, you? You stupid underclassman, I've got the edge." His brogue-tinged voice rang out in triumphant glee. "I'm still twenty years old—look at you! You're an old man!"

Kirk rolled to his feet and swung. Finnegan ducked, slipped and landed hard. Kirk allowed himself a moment to savor this victory.

"Uh—uh," grunted the prostrate cadet. "Jim! I can't move my legs. Ohhh. Me back, it's broken. You've broken me back . . . Ohhhh!"

Officer and Gentleman. Kirk knelt and carefully straightened his victim's leg. He palpated muscle. Finnegan groaned and shook his head dizzily. Kirk moved closer and probed cautiously. "Can you feel that?"

And he fell flat as Finnegan's clasped hands landed on the nape of his neck in a mighty double chop. Finnegan leaped to his feet, laughing.

" 'Can you feel that?' " he mocked. "Sleep sweet, Jimmy boy. Sleep as long as you like. Sleep forever, Jimmy boy, forever and ever . . ."

Kirk was not in a position to appreciate this ironic lullaby. Watery images vaguely swam before his eyes, his nose hurt, and the back of his head was resting on a sharp pebble.

Finnegan loomed above him against the sky, hands resting on his hips, shaking his head sadly.

"Won't you ever learn, Jim boy? You never could take me!"

Kirk painfully propped himself up on one elbow and spat blood. He wheezed, "Finnegan. One thing."

Magnanimous, Finnegan said, "Sure, name it."

"Answers!"

He should have known better.

"Earn 'em!"

As he started groggily to his feet, Finnegan floored him again.

He lay there for one minute. This had gone too far. Fair or foul, the swaggering hooligan was going to get it. He rolled over, and, summoning all his unarmed-combat training, got on his feet in the same motion. Finnegan gestured, come on, come on, from his defen-

sive crouch. ". . . wipe that grin off his face," Kirk
thought, as he lunged. He landed a crunching blow
and Finnegan reeled, recovered and came back.

It seemed hours of bruising impacts on rib, jaw,
arms. It was harder and harder to lift the hand and
push it through the air, which had become harder
and harder to breathe. Finally, Kirk pounded his last
remaining strength into Finnegan's midriff, and the
man dropped and lay still. Kirk fell back against the
rock and tried to breathe. He had thought he was exhausted before. And he didn't dare close his eyes to
blink away the running sweat, lest Finnegan be playing
possum again. And he just could not lift his arms.

Finnegan came to, slowly. "Not bad," he said grudg-
ingly.

"Yeah."

"Kinda . . . ow! Makes up for things, huh, Jim?"

Kirk licked blood off his lip. "A lot of things." Even
if he had a black eye. "Now, what has been happening
to my people?"

With a touch of his old arrogance, Finnegan smirked.
"I never answer questions from Plebes."

"I'm not a plebe. This is *today*, fifteen years later.
What are you doing here?"

There was a pause as they looked at each other.

"Being exactly what you expect me to be, Jim boy!"
cried Finnegan as he threw a handful of dirt in Kirk's
eyes and scrambled to his feet. Kirk lost his balance
but landed with one fist heavy in Finnegan's solar
plexus. Finnegan closed with him.

Swaying like a couple of drunks with tiredness,
neither would give in. But Finnegan wasn't laughing
anymore. He'd started dodging Kirk's blows. Kirk
thought, he's twenty years old, and he's winded—more
winded than the old man! He evaded a wide swing and
grabbed a handful of Finnegan's tunic, driving his fist
right into the bully's battered face with a final, ex-
plosive grunt.

And that was definitely that. Finnegan was out for

the count. And Kirk, breathless, bruised and bleeding, felt like crowing. After all these years . . .

As he felt a grin painfully stretching his cut lip, Spock said, "Did you enjoy it, Captain?"

"Yes," panted Kirk, gloating. "I did enjoy it. For almost half my lifetime, the one thing I wanted was to beat the tar out of Finnegan."

Spock raised his right eyebrow. "This supports a theory I have been formulating . . ."

"We're all meeting people and things we happen to be thinking about at the moment."

Spock nodded. "Somehow our thoughts are read, then that object is quickly manufactured and provided."

"H'm. So it gets dangerous if we happen to be thinking about—" Kirk stopped hastily.

"We must control our thoughts carefully." Spock, of course, would not find this difficult.

Kirk tried not to think about—no! or . . . not *that,* either!

"The power field we detected is undoubtedly underground, fabricating these things. Passages lead up to the surface. As, for example, when Rodriguez thought of a tiger—" Even Spock was not infallible, it seemed. There was a snarling roar, and the magnificent head of a Bengal tiger peered at them over the rocks. It padded over the ridge and down out of sight among the shrubs—toward them.

Without moving, Kirk eyed the bushes. "We've got to get back to the others and warn them."

Spock, immobile, murmured, "Yes."

"We have to get out of here."

"Immediately, Captain."

They looked at each other sidewise. "You go first, Spock. I'll try and distract him."

"I can't let you do that, sir. I'll distract him." The tiger waited patiently for them to make the first move. It waited, crouching, then settled down. It began to lick its paws.

"We could try moving very slowly."

With extreme caution, Kirk extended a foot. The tiger watched interestedly. He leaned weight on the foot and achieved a step. Spock glided beside him as they edged around the rock. They ran like hell.

Behind them, the tiger turned itself off.

Rodriguez fell out of the shrubbery in their path. "Angela! The plane—" On cue, the Sopwith Camel appeared overhead in mid-dive. Kirk threw himself and his men to the ground as 50-caliber machine-gun bullets plowed the path at their side.

"Don't think about it!" said Kirk. "To the glade, fast!"

"Hai!" The Japanese warrior in his heavy complex armor flailed at them with a sharp sword. "Ahh-HOU!" But he was hampered by his carapace, and they dodged him easily.

As they reached the glade, Yeoman Barrows seemed to be in difficulties again. Sulu was wrestling with the bearded amorist in the black cloak as she clutched her tattered tunic in front of her; apparently she had been changing out of her princess's dress when accosted.

But Don Juan melted away as Kirk and Spock pelted up to them.

"Sulu, Rodriguez, Barrows—front and center!" snapped Kirk.

"Sir—"

"Don't ask any questions. This is an order!" They moved in to face him, Tonia squirming into her uniform.

"Now brace. Everyone, eyes front. Don't talk. Don't breathe. Don't think. You're at attention and concentrating on that and only that. Concentrate!"

The three crewmen obediently struggled not to think.

Spock gestured, and Kirk turned to see a new apparition. A kindly old gentleman in dignified robes smiled at him.

"Who are you?" From whose errant thoughts had this one appeared?

"I am the Caretaker of this planet, Captain Kirk."

"You know me?"

"But of course." He nodded toward the bewildered crewmen. "And Lieutenant Rodriguez, Lieutenant Sulu, Yeoman Barrows—and Mr. Spock."

The dangers in this place had not, so far, appeared in sheep's clothing. They had been all obvious threats. Perhaps . . .

"I stopped by to check our power supplies, and have only just realized that we had guests who did not understand all this. These experiences were intended to amuse you."

Kirk was taken aback. *"Amuse* us! Is that your word for all we've been through?"

The man laughed easily. "Oh, none of this is permanent." He waved at the surrounding glade, the forest, the meadows. "Here you have merely to imagine your fondest wishes—old ones you wish to relive, new ones, battle, fear, love, triumph. Anything which pleases you can be made to happen here."

"The term," said Spock, out of the encyclopedia he housed in his brain, "is 'amusement park.' "

"But of course." The Caretaker sounded as though this were perfectly obvious.

"An old Earth term for a place where people could go to see and do all kinds of exciting and fantastic things."

"This planet was constructed for our race of people, Captain. We come here, and play."

Sulu was puzzled. "Play? As advanced as you are, and you still play?"

The Caretaker looked at him pityingly. Kirk waved Sulu to silence. "Play, Mr. Sulu. The more complex the mind, the greater the need for the simplicity of play."

The robed figure beamed approvingly. "Exactly, Captain. You are most perceptive.

"I regret that your equipment was inadvertently affected. The system needed slight adjustment—it was pulling energy from the nearest available source. I think you will find that all is now in order."

But it hadn't been all play. The fight with Finnegan had been extremely satisfying; the tiger had, after all, harmed no one; and Tonia's virtue was still intact. But . . .

"None of this explains the death of my ship's surgeon," said Kirk. The "amusement park" of an advanced race had turned killer for the younger people. The Caretaker's face was gentle and his words reassuring, but perhaps the toys of his race were too dangerous.

"Possibly because I haven't died, Jim," said McCoy's voice behind him. Yeoman Barrows turned pale, and then radiant with joy.

McCoy sauntered into the clearing, in the pink of health, with a young lady clad in a few feathers clinging to each of his arms.

"I was taken below the surface," he explained, glancing at his chest, "for some rather—remarkable —repairs. It's amazing! There's a factory complex down there like nothing I've ever seen. They can build anything—immediately!"

Tonia had run to him, and was gazing into his face as if she could not believe her eyes. She touched his chest, last seen torn and bleeding. She became conscious of an obstruction and belatedly realized that McCoy was not alone.

She found her tongue. "And how do you explain *them?*"

"Er—" McCoy glanced fondly at the two voluptuous, bare, willing beauties on his arms. "Well, I was thinking about a little cabaret I know on Rigel II. There were these two girls in the chorus line that I— well—" his assurance faltered. "Er—here they are."

Tonia looked. He said, "Well, after all, I am on shore leave."

"So am I," said Tonia ominously.

"Er—" McCoy would just have to spread himself around. "So you are."

Yeoman Barrows waited.

Resigning himself to the not-unattractive inevitable, McCoy released the charmers. "Well, girls, I'm sure you can turn something up."

The girls smiled a cheerful farewell to the doctor and moved. To Sulu's evident delight, the redhead chose to nestle up to him. Spock, however, did not appear gratified at the armful of blonde that approached him. He dodged politely, but to no avail. She insinuated herself somehow and stood alarmingly close.

Rodriguez said, very quietly, "And—Angela?"

"Esteban!" she said, hurrying out of the shrubbery. "I've been looking all over for you!" He took her hand and stared, unbelievingly.

The Caretaker smiled upon all these couples, even at the restive Spock. "We regret that you have been made uncomfortable, even puzzled."

Kirk had relaxed enough to be curious. "You say your people built this? Who are you? What planet are you from?"

The Caretaker shook his white head. "Your race is not yet ready to understand us, Captain Kirk."

Spock, still trying to tactfully disentangle himself from the cabaret girl, replied, "I tend to agree."

The communicator beeped. "This is the bridge, Captain. Our power systems have come back in. Do you require any assistance?"

"Everything is in order, Lieutenant Uhura. Stand by." It seemed now that everything was indeed in order. But . . .

"With the proper caution, our amusement planet could be an ideal place for your people to enjoy themselves, if you wish," said the Caretaker.

McCoy, now firmly attached to Yeoman Barrows, said, "It *is* what the doctor ordered, Jim."

"Very well . . . Bridge! I'll be sending up a short briefing. As soon as all personnel have heard it, you may commence transporting shore parties. And tell them to prepare for the best shore leave they've ever had!"

As Kirk shut his communicator, Mr. Spock approached him, still surrounded by pink feathers and bare legs. "I'll go back aboard, Captain. With all due respect to the young lady, I've had about all the shore leave I care for."

The young lady, acknowledging defeat, joined her companion. Sulu did not seem to mind.

"No, Mr. Spock, I'll go. You—"

Ruth glided out from the forest canopy and held out her hands, smiling.

"On the other hand, perhaps I'll stay for a day or two . . ." said the Captain, leaving Spock to his own devices.

Later, Spock greeted them, impassive as ever. He shook his head as he looked at their suntanned faces.

"Enjoy your shore leave, gentlemen?"

Kirk met McCoy's amused eye. "That we did, Mr. Spock. That we did!"

Spock stared at them, puzzled. They seemed full of satisfaction. He shrugged.

"Most illogical," he said with finality.

The *Enterprise* departed at Warp Factor One amid the guffaws of the Captain and the ship's surgeon.

APPENDIX I

STAR TREK TITLES

AUTHORS

Star Trek 1

Balance of Terror	Paul Schneider
Charlie's Law (Charlie X)	Teleplay by D. C. Fontana
	Story by Gene Roddenberry
Conscience of the King, The	Barry Trivers
Dagger of the Mind	S. Bar-David
Man Trap (The Unreal McCoy)	George Clayton Johnson
Miri	Adrian Spies
Naked Time, The	John D. F. Black

Star Trek 2

Arena	Gene L. Coon
City on the Edge of Forever, The	Harlan Ellison
Court Martial	Don M. Mankiewicz and Steven W. Carabatsos
Errand of Mercy	Gene L. Coon
Operation—Annihilate!	Steven W. Carabatsos
Space Seed	Carey Wilber and Gene L. Coon
Taste of Armageddon, A	Robert Hammer and Gene L. Coon
Tomorrow Is Yesterday	D. C. Fontana

Star Trek 3

Amok Time	Theodore Sturgeon
Assignment: Earth	Gene Roddenberry and Art Wallace

171

STAR TREK TITLES	AUTHORS
Doomsday Machine, The	Norman Spinrad
Friday's Child	D. C. Fontana
Last Gunfight, The	Lee Cronin
(The OK Corral)	
Mirror, Mirror	Jerome Bixby
Trouble with Tribbles, The	David Gerrold

Star Trek 4

All Our Yesterdays	Jean Lisette Aroeste
Devil in the Dark, The	Gene L. Coon
Enterprise Incident, The	D. C. Fontana
Journey to Babel	D. C. Fontana
Menagerie, The	Gene Roddenberry
Piece of the Action, A	David P. Harmon and Gene L. Coon

Star Trek 5

Let That Be Your Last Battlefield	Oliver Crawford and Lee Cronin
Requiem for Methuselah	Jerome Bixby
This Side of Paradise	Nathan Butler and D. C. Fontana
Tholian Web, The	Judy Burns and Chet Richards
Turnabout Intruder	Gene Roddenberry and Arthur H. Singer
Way to Eden, The	Arthur Heinemann and Michael Richards
Whom Gods Destroy	Lee Erwin and Jerry Sohl

Star Trek 6

Apple, The	Max Ehrlich and Gene L. Coon
By Any Other Name	D. C. Fontana and Jerome Bixby
Cloud Minders, The	Margaret Armen, David Gerrold and Oliver Crawford
Lights of Zetar, The	Jeremy Tarcher and Shari Lewis

STAR TREK TITLES	AUTHORS
Mark of Gideon, The	George F. Slavin and Stanley Adams
Savage Curtain, The	Gene Roddenberry and Arthur Heinemann

Star Trek 7

Changeling, The	John Meredyth Lucas
Deadly Years, The	David P. Harmon
Elaan of Troyius	John Meredyth Lucas
Metamorphosis	Gene L. Coon
Paradise Syndrome, The	Margaret Armen
Who Mourns for Adonais	Gilbert A. Ralston and Gene L. Coon

Star Trek 8

Catspaw	Robert Bloch
Enemy Within, The	Richard Matheson
For the World Is Hollow and I Have Touched the Sky	Rik Vollaerts
Spock's Brain	Lee Cronin
Where No Man Has Gone Before	Samuel A. Peeples
Wolf in the Fold	Robert Bloch

Star Trek 9

Immunity Syndrome, The	Robert Sabaroff
Obsession	Art Wallace
Return of the Archons, The	Boris Sobelman
Return to Tomorrow	Gene Roddenberry and John T. Dugan
That Which Survives	John Meredyth Lucas and D. C. Fontana
Ultimate Computer, The	D. C. Fontana and Laurence N. Wolfe

Star Trek 10

Alternative Factor, The	Don Ingalls
Empath, The	Joyce Muskat
Galileo Seven, The	Simon Wincelberg and Oliver Crawford
Is There in Truth No Beauty?	Jean Lisette Aroeste

STAR TREK TITLES	AUTHORS
Omega Glory, The	Gene Roddenberry
Private Little War, A	Don Ingalls and
	Gene Roddenberry

Star Trek 11

Bread and Circuses	Gene Roddenberry and
	Gene L. Coon
Day of the Dove	Jerome Bixby
Plato's Stepchildren	Meyer Dolinsky
Squire of Gothos, The	Paul Schneider
What Are Little Girls Made Of?	Robert Bloch
Wink of an Eye	Arthur Heinemann and
	Lee Cronin

Star Trek 12

And the Children Shall Lead*	Edward J. Lakso
Corbomite Maneuver, The	Jerry Sohl
Gamesters of Triskelion, The	Margaret Armen
Patterns of Force	John Meredyth Lucas
Shore Leave*	Theodore Sturgeon

---

*Adapted by J. A. Lawrence.

APPENDIX II

NOTES

Seasons: First: September 1966–April 1967
              Second: September 1967–April 1968
              Third: September 1968–April 1969

"I, Mudd" and "Mudd's Women" will appear soon in an expanded version.

STAR TREK TITLES
(Alphabetical)

Title	Collection Number	Season
All Our Yesterdays	4	3
Alternative Factor, The	10	1
Amok Time	3	2
And the Children Shall Lead	12	3
Apple, The	6	2
Arena	2	1
Assignment: Earth	3	2
Balance of Terror	1	1
Bread and Circuses	11	2
By Any Other Name	6	2
Catspaw	8	2
Changeling, The	7	2
Charlie's Law (Charlie X)	1	1
City on the Edge of Forever, The	2	1
Cloud Minders, The	6	3
Conscience of the King, The	1	1
Corbomite Maneuver, The	12	1
Court Martial	2	1
Dagger of the Mind	1	1

Title	Collection Number	Season
Day of the Dove	11	3
Deadly Years, The	7	2
Devil in the Dark, The	4	1
Doomsday Machine, The	3	2
Elaan of Troyius	7	3
Empath, The	10	3
Enemy Within, The	8	1
Enterprise Incident, The	4	3
Errand of Mercy	2	1
For the World Is Hollow and I Have Touched the Sky	8	3
Friday's Child	3	2
Galileo Seven, The	10	1
Gamesters of Triskelion, The	12	2
Immunity Syndrome, The	9	2
I, Mudd	see notes	2
Is There in Truth No Beauty?	10	3
Journey to Babel	4	2
Last Gunfight, The (The OK Corral)	3	3
Let That Be Your Last Battlefield	5	3
Lights of Zetar, The	6	3
Man Trap (The Unreal McCoy)	1	1
Mark of Gideon, The	6	2
Menagerie, The	4	1
Metamorphosis	7	2
Miri	1	1
Mirror, Mirror	3	2
Mudd's Women	see notes	1
Naked Time, The	1	1
Obsession	9	2
Omega Glory, The	10	2
Operation—Annihilate!	2	1
Paradise Syndrome, The	7	3
Patterns of Force	12	2
Piece of the Action, A	4	2
Plato's Stepchildren	11	3
Private Little War, A	10	2
Requiem for Methuselah	5	3
Return of the Archons, The	9	1
Return to Tomorrow	9	2
Savage Curtain The	6	3
Shore Leave	12	1
Space Seed	2	1
Spock Must Die!	original novel	not broadcast

Title	Collection Number	Season
Spock's Brain	8	3
Squire of Gothos, The	11	1
Taste of Armageddon, A	2	1
That Which Survives	9	3
This Side of Paradise	5	1
Tholian Web, The	5	3
Tomorrow Is Yesterday	2	1
Trouble with Tribbles, The	3	2
Turnabout Intruder	5	3
Ultimate Computer, The	9	2
Unreal McCoy, The (see Man Trap)		
Way to Eden, The	5	3
What Are Little Girls Made Of?	11	1
Where No Man Has Gone Before	8	1
Who Mourns for Adonais?	7	2
Whom Gods Destroy	5	3
Wink of an Eye	11	3
Wolf in the Fold	8	2

STAR TREK 9
Adapted by JAMES BLISH

Join Captain James Kirk, together with First Officer Spock, Doctor 'Bones' McCoy and Chief Engineer 'Scotty', as they, with the rest of the crew of the Starship *USS Enterprise*, continue their hazardous journey into space.

On this mission, they exchange bodies with an alien intelligence; engage in deadly war games; pursue a vaporous creature to a desolate planet; and probe a fearsome zone of darkness that threatens to destroy them all . . .

0 552 09476 5   £1.50

STAR TREK 10
Adapted by JAMES BLISH

The *USS Enterprise* continues its journey across the thresholds of space. As it hurtles through light-years of uncharted space the crew are faced with a ravening, murderous monster aboard the Starship, whose only instinct is to destroy; Captain Kirk discovers an incredibly beautiful creature with strange powers of healing; and First Officer Spock risks insanity when he views the forbidden Kollos . . .

0 552 09553 2   £1.50

STAR TREK 11
by JAMES BLISH

The Starship *USS Enterprise* continues its hazardous journey across the thresholds of space, carrying Captain James Kirk, First Officer Spock, Doctor 'Bones' McCoy and Chief Engineer 'Scotty' into the perilous unknown of the universe . . .

In STAR TREK 11, Captain Kirk is trapped on a planet ruled by androids, the crew of the *Enterprise* are entertained by an eighteenth century squire in a deadly game of charades, and the Starship is invaded by an alien entity who feeds on hate . . .

0 552 09850 7   £1.50

DEVIL WORLD
by GORDON EKLUND

The Starship *USS Enterprise* carries Captain Kirk and his crew to Heartland . . . a mysterious planet populated by a small but terrifying race of demonic beings.

Heartland . . . where Captain Kirk falls in love with a beautiful, mysterious woman with a fatal secret.

Heartland . . . where Kirk, Spock and the rest of the crew will be challenged by an awesome disembodied intelligence, more powerful than any other force in the universe.

0 552 12580 6   £1.50

STAR TREK TITLES AVAILABLE
FROM CORGI BOOKS

WHILE EVERY EFFORT IS MADE TO KEEP PRICES LOW, IT IS
SOMETIMES NECESSARY TO INCREASE PRICES AT SHORT NOTICE.
CORGI BOOKS RESERVE THE RIGHT TO SHOW NEW RETAIL PRICES ON
COVERS WHICH MAY DIFFER FROM THOSE PREVIOUSLY ADVERTISED
IN THE TEXT OR ELSEWHERE.

THE PRICES SHOWN BELOW WERE CORRECT AT THE TIME OF GOING
TO PRESS (JANUARY '85).

☐	09080 8	STAR TREK 1	James Blish	£1.50
☐	09081 6	STAR TREK 2	James Blish	£1.50
☐	09082 4	STAR TREK 3	James Blish	£1.50
☐	09445 5	STAR TREK 4	James Blish	£1.50
☐	09446 3	STAR TREK 5	James Blish	£1.50
☐	09447 1	STAR TREK 6	James Blish	£1.50
☐	09229 0	STAR TREK 7	James Blish	£1.50
☐	09289 4	STAR TREK 8	James Blish	£1.50
☐	09476 5	STAR TREK 9	James Blish	£1.50
☐	09553 2	STAR TREK 10	James Blish	£1.50
☐	09850 7	STAR TREK 11	James Blish	£1.50
☐	10281 4	SPOCK MESSIAH	James Blish	£1.50
☐	09498 6	SPOCK MUST DIE	James Blish	£1.50
☐	12581 4	THE STARLESS WORLD	Gordon Eklund	£1.50
☐	12580 6	DEVIL WORLD	Gordon Eklund	£1.50
☐	12431 1	TREK TO MAD WORLD	Stephen Goldin	£1.50
☐	10865 0	MUDD'S ANGELS: A STAR TREK NOVEL	J. A. Lawrence	75p
☐	01083 2	STAR TREK INTERGALACTIC PUZZLES	James Razzi	£1.95
☐	12582 2	VULCAN!	Kathleen Sky	£1.50

*All these books are available at your book shop or newsagent, or can be ordered
direct from the publisher. Just tick the titles you want and fill in the form below.*

CORGI BOOKS, Cash Sales Department, P.O. Box 11, Falmouth, Cornwall.

Please send cheque or postal order, no currency.

Please allow cost of book(s) plus the following for postage and packing:

U.K. Customers—Allow 55p for the first book, 22p for the second book and 14p for
each additional book ordered, to a maximum charge of £1.75.

B.F.P.O. and Eire—Allow 55p for the first book, 22p for the second book plus 14p
per copy for the next seven books, thereafter 8p per book.

Overseas Customers—Allow £1.00 for the first book and 25p per copy for each
additional book.

NAME (Block Letters) ....

ADDRESS ....

....